THE PLUTONUS CELL: PATH TO FREEDOM

SUE STRALEY

Strategic Book Publishing
New York, NewYork

Copyright 2008
All rights reserved – Sue Straley

No part of this book may be reproduced or transmitted in any form or by any means, graphic, electronic, or mechanical, including photocopying, recording, taping, or by any information storage retrieval system, without the permission, in writing, from the publisher.

Strategic Book Publishing
An imprint of AEG Publishing Group
845 Third Avenue, 6th Floor - 6016
New York, NY 10022
www.StrategicBookPublishing.com

ISBN 978-1-60693-714-3   1-60693-714-6

Printed in the United States of America

Book Design: Linda W. Rigsbee

PREFACE

BEFORE THERE was a colony on Pretoria, everyone lived on Plutonus and it was wired and wild, full of bustling factories. After many decades of waste and pollution the world's population had to enter domes, and all vegetation died from the toxic air. The problem reached a critical condition and the government explored other worlds in an effort to find a solution to the problem.

The reports received explained that Pretoria was the perfect planet to use for food growth. The leaders of Plutonus decided to colonize Pretoria and made it a farming and education colony. They had learned from their past mistakes, and the laws on Pretoria were strict. All factories would use alternative fuel sources and follow strict filtration policies. They wouldn't allow anyone but government officials to have cars and they had to be electric. All cities were encased in domes that used only solar panels for power.

From birth, the colonists of Pretoria received mandatory training for specific careers. Citizens were hand picked based on early testing and they continued their education at the new training center. The government had it set up to limit the traffic in and out of Pretoria. Only specific military or government transports returned to Plutonus. The food grown on Pretoria shipped in automated cargo transports that were recovered by cruisers in space. Much of the population on Pretoria had never been to the homeland of Plutonus. Only the few who'd served under the government had been to there.

A large body of the population felt as if they were slaves—they couldn't see or visit Plutonus. Under the current laws, if a citizen invented or developed a new idea, they could complete the rough work, then it would be taken to be produced on Plutonus. The government rarely compensated these inventors, thus the rise of the alliance to help the inventors keep their inventions and help finish them before the government heard. The alliance dedicated their cause to giving credit where deserved. Until recently, the alliance was a peaceful organization. Most of the members of held some type of office of importance—doctors, teachers, and select government officials.

A splinter cell formed from the alliance had begun to get very violent; they wanted swifter changes. They had begun attacking government offices, as well as transports into Plutonus. A number of top leaders in the alliance had formed together to search and expose the cell. They sent a select number of undercover agents to infiltrate the cell. To date, the cell had been able to detect the undercover agents. A few made it farther than the others, but communication had been lost when the violence increased. Discreet signs have been recently passed, acknowledging the infiltration of the top ranks. They won't back down now.

CHAPTER 1

ARON GABRIELS was shaken from his thoughts by the constant ringing of the phone that he refused to answer, knowing who was on the other end of line. He put his head in his hands, gingerly fingering the bandage across his right temple, and gave a frustrated groan. The day had started out with an air of expectation. A group of state officials, including the provincial governor, had come to inspect a new crop harvesting transport. The group had a tour of the machine and was in agreement that it would vastly improve crop picking capabilities.

The harvester had just finished its demonstration and was leaving the atmosphere. There was a loud explosion as they looked toward the sky. Screams could be heard from every direction as a hailstorm of orange flame and debris rained down from the exploding harvester. There was pandemonium while everyone was trying to scramble for cover. People trampled the many injured or dead, but there was no cover in the open field. Debris showered down for miles around in great big chunks, injuring numerous by-standers and state officials.

Aron could still hear the screams, see the bloody gashes, and feel the sheer terror. Ambulance transports couldn't fly safely through the falling debris, and emergency ground crews had to be called in to put out the fires. It was a sight he would never forget—the image would forever be etched in his mind. After hours of questioning by Military Intel, he returned to his office to find a dozen messages from other alliance members who wanted to know what happened. They were calling for swift action and no excuses.

Government officials were blaming the alliance, but Aron knew differently. He was their leader and would never order something this destructive. The thought of it made him sick. Their mission started over twenty years earlier when the home planet of Plutonus passed a law stating that all incomplete inventions would be claimed by the government and completed on Plutonus.

Pretoria's environment also possessed unique gene altering effects on unborn children. Many of the children have escaped detection but the ones who hadn't were sent to Plutonus. The alliance has begun their own tracking system for gifted colonists, and the list has been kept secret so far. They feared for their children and would do anything to protect them.

The rise of the alliance assisted inventors in keeping their creations, helped them finish them before the government intervened, and protected the gifted children. Until recently, the alliance had been peaceful. Most of the members hold some type of office of importance—doctors, teachers, lawyers, and select government officials. They are dedicated to protecting all the citizens of Pretoria.

In the last year a splinter cell has started to get very violent, attacking government offices and transports into Plutonus. The explosion was the latest in several months. Each attack is more violent than the one before it, and more lives are lost each time. The police have a growing list of unsolved murders to add to the woes of the alliance, some of which are the murders of top officials.

The leaders of the Alliance have banned together to search and expose the cell. They have sent undercover agents to infiltrate the cell and eliminate their leader. To date, the cell seems to have detected most of the undercover agents, and only a few of them have made it close to the cell in recent months. Communication has been lost, but discreet signs have been passed to acknowledge the infiltration.

Aron has contacted one of the best operatives, Robert Michaels. The only way the alliance can continue its work is by breaking the cell as quickly as possible, and Michaels is the best man for the job. He recruited Michaels five years ago when he realized his potential as an operative. From the intelligence Aron had gathered, Michaels was retired from the military and had been a master at infiltration during his enlistment. He was currently working close to the leaders, and Aron has been unable to contact him through normal channels.

Aron feared for Michael's safety and couldn't help thinking that he'd been found out. He broke from his musing and picked up the phone to call a meeting of the top alliance members. The cell had to be stopped.

CHAPTER 2

IT WAS a typical mid-summer day in the dome on Pretoria. Sam Gabriels was on her way to the training center in East Luella for another round of classes. She had been working toward her political science degree and was entering her last year. Sam had planned to follow in her fathers' footsteps and become a government leader.

As she walked across the quad to the transit pods, Sam saw the provincial police who always targeted the passages and intimidated the women. Sam headed through the security checkpoint where passengers were being searched for contraband by military officers. She flashed her credentials flippantly, and scoffed at the thought of how bad it would be if they ever found out whom her father *really* was. One of the officers whistled to Sam. "Sam! When are we going out?"

"Only in your dreams," she said, and waved the comment off. Sam was used to it. They started when she was thirteen and reached her full height and her hair turned a fiery red. That afternoon, she had joined her best friends Nick and Niles McGovens on a tour of the Luella Police Station with their dad, the chief. Ever since then, a day doesn't go by without a remark or a leering look.

"We've missed you at the station. Don't keep us waiting to long to see your beautiful face," Sam just glared at him and he put a hand to his chest. "You wound me." His fellow officers laughed and moved on down the station.

As Sam waited on the platform, she spotted a guy who was standing alone on the other side, watching the crowd. He was dressed in ragged faded jeans, a long sleeve shirt. He was sporting a dark black beard, and had a ragged cloak draped over one arm. He looked way out of place. His eyes connected with hers for just a second and her stomach did a little flip.

The pod came into the station and she climbed on, noticing that the tattered young man stayed behind. She wondered why, because the next pod out only went down to a very rough part of town. Her father told her how rough it was there, and that they fight for a place to sleep in the alley. The man had a certain quality that didn't fit with the image. Part of her studies was learning how to read people.

Sam reached the station for the training center and headed to class. She saw a large crowd near the campus bulletin board and wondered what was happening. The crowd was rambling about the leader of the Republic coming to Pretoria to meet with the leaders of the police and Citizens Assimilation Re-education Task Force (CART). Legislation was being discussed regarding CART's treatment of prisoners and the conditions of the mines. The officials weren't enthused with the proposed changes. They were formed to re-educate those who fight against government policy and rebel through violence. Changing CART would send a message to citizens that punishment was no longer an option and to go ahead and do their worst.

Sam knew her father would love the news of the upcoming event, as he was against the change. She continued on to her classes, starting with Governmental Science and couldn't wait for her final year to be done. When she graduated, she could finally focus on her career goals and make life better for the citizens of Pretoria. Her internship program was on the fast track and moving faster by the day.

Sam looked just like her picture. She wasn't hard to miss with her fiery red hair, sparkling emerald eyes, and long legs. She was wearing her school uniform, a short black skirt and white top. She had tied the ends together at her waist, causing her belly button to show. There was a tiny gold piercing to top it off. It's a shame he had to involve her. Sam's father had been out of touch and he couldn't risk contacting his cousin—not after the transporter incident. He'd have to wait for the right moment to approach her. One never could tell who was watching or who to trust. He could always pass the information to his cousin through other channels, but there was no guarantee it wouldn't be intercepted. He couldn't risk being seen with him; too many people would question it. They already suspected him after their most recent request he'd denied. If he could just get close enough to Aron's home undetected, he may not have to involve his daughter.

After her classes, Sam headed back to the pod station and as she waited, she noticed the tattered young man. She was much closer to him this time. She took in his appearance, his right eye was artificially enhanced, one of the expensive ones from the army. He had an odd tattoo on his left wrist that peeked out from under his shirtsleeve. He had long black hair that was tucked into the hood of his cloak. She waited and as she watched him, questions swam around in her mind. Was he was waiting for someone? Her answer came quickly. The young man got on, rode to her stop, exited, and headed in the opposite direction.

As Sam headed off, she wondered what her father had been up to all day. He worked as the local provincial mayor for the City of Luella. When she reached home, her father was arguing with her mother. She yelled, "I'm home!" and headed up to her room where she'd change clothes and start her studies. Homework, she knew, was essential. She longed for real life knowledge.

After a while, her father came in and kissed her forehead. He said, "I have to leave town for a few days, but I'll be back soon. Don't forget your training." He shook a finger at her when she started to protest.

As he walked down the hallway, Sam complained. "How could I forget? Where are you going?" She reached out her hand to stop his progress and noticed the bandage. "When did this happen?" she asked, concern lighting her face.

He had to tell her the truth; she wouldn't let him leave otherwise. Sam was the only one he really trusted besides his wife. "There was an explosion this morning," he stated grimly.

"The cell?" she questioned with an expectant light in her eyes.

"Yes. Don't look at me like that, you shouldn't even know about them." He started to leave again. She halted him with a touch of her hand.

"Shouldn't you stay here?" she asked.

A frown crossed his face as he touched the bandage. "No, I have to take care of some pressing matters for work. I'm going to the Capital Mantis to meet with the governor."

"Wait. Did you know that the leader of the Republic is coming to meet with CART?" Sam asked, catching up to her father as he turned to leave.

He smiled and said, "I did. Now, I have to be on my way. Be

careful this weekend." He placed a hand to her cheek. Sam sensed the tension in her father's voice and touch. She was nervous; things were never good when he took that tone.

Across the street from the Gabriels house a silent observer waited and listened. What's this? The mayor was leaving town. What matter of business could be so urgent? Doesn't he realize it's not safe? The cell has become unpredictable, and this latest attack only adds to the danger. He should stay near his family and protect them. If he left town now, he'd never be able to reach him. His frustration mounted as he followed Aron intent on passing the disk to him before he left town.

Under the cover of night, five darkly clad figures met in the private back room of the Chez Ramey restaurant in Mantis. Each man arrived separately at the summons of the fifth member and leader. There was an air of sorrow surrounding the members. Two of them were present at the explosion. Their leader, Aron Gabriels, was last to speak and he told them of the tragedy outside Luella, detail by detail leaving nothing out. He explained how Military Intel had been looking into the alliance as a possible scapegoat for everything that had happened. He tried to lead them in another direction and focus their attention elsewhere.

"What are we going to do?" one member asked as she sipped at a glass of wine with shaking hands.

"How are we going get out of this?" another member asked with a groan of frustration. Aron had been running that thought through his own mind. The answer would depend on their actions.

"I told you, we have an operative inside the cell. He's going to get the evidence we need to take them down," Aron quickly answered.

"Can we trust him?" The provincial governor took a sip of whisky, waited for Aron to answer, and watched the other members.

Aron looked directly into his eyes and responded with conviction. "Absolutely. I'd trust him with my life. He's the best at what he does; I recruited him myself. He's been working inside for four years now and has never failed."

"What plan of action do you have in mind?" the governor casually asked as he broke off a piece of bread and popped it into his mouth.

"We need to find out who the leader is first, and then remove him or her," Aron slumped in his chair and looked around at his friends. "Any move now could alert them and we'd lose our chance. They could turn the tables on us."

"I don't like the idea of killing anyone. How do you plan on removing them?" one of the members came to his feet and started toward Aron.

Aron got up to intercept and put his hand on the members shoulder. "Calm down. Take your seat. I'm not talking about killing anyone. There are other ways of removing someone. CART can be very useful to us. They don't look kindly on traitors and frown on any form of treason."

"I've heard horror stories about CART. People go in, but they don't leave." He squirmed in his chair and remembered the details a military officer told him once.

"They have a certain way of dealing with prisoners. Our inside man is currently searching for hard evidence. He is confident someone will slip up and have a disk containing all the information we need."

"How soon will we know if he has succeeded?" the governor inquired, coolly toying with his fork.

"I don't know," Aron said with a sigh. "Look, I've been unable to reach him. I took a risk coming here today; I have a suspicion I'm being watched. We have to be careful who we give information to from this point on."

The provincial governor sat up at the statement. "What do you mean?" His eyes grew wide with curiosity, gone was his cool and aloft manner.

Aron looked directly at the governor and repeated his request. "I mean don't tell anyone why you were at this restaurant, or what we discussed. We're the only ones who can know."

"My wife and my assistant know where I am, but not why. She thinks I'm having a late dinner with friends," he said nonchalantly.

"Keep it that way, and watch your back when you leave. Are we all agreed that the leader needs to be exposed and handed over to CART?" Aron surveyed the faces before him. They all nodded in agreement and one by one they left.

The next morning Aron's phone rang and he frowned at the name displayed. *Why would the provincial governors assistant, Lynn Weston, need to speak to me?* he thought. He shrugged his shoulders and answered. "Hello?"

"Do you think we could meet this afternoon, Mayor Gabriels?" She sounded close to tears and Aron cautiously asked his question.

"What do you need to meet with me about?" He was concerned something was very wrong now as he heard her sobs.

"The provincial governor was murdered last night. I don't know what to do. The police are asking all sorts of questions. I know he had a late dinner meeting with you. I thought you might be able to help straighten out a few things. Please, will you meet with me?" She sounded desperate.

Aron was shocked, and was having a hard time speaking. The news hit him hard. The provincial governor was a dear friend from college, and he just visited with him the night before. He stammered, "Of course I'll meet with you. Just tell me when and where."

"My office is across from the Hotel Dirtron. Say, about four o'clock?"

"I'll be there." He sank down in the chair holding his head in his hands. Questions swirled in his mind, causing it to ache painfully. The cell had made the first move; he vowed to make the last.

CHAPTER 3

SAM WAS awakened by voices outside her window. There were three policemen talking. She was within earshot as she learned that the provincial governor of Mantis was killed. All they found was a small hole at the base of his neck, and a puddle of blood. The local police had no idea what type of weapon was used and were calling in Military Intel. Sam was startled by what she heard, and hastily took off to meet her friends for their usual Saturday out. Sam was in such a hurry she almost forgot her training workout. She heard her father's reminder rattle through her head. "Samantha," he said, "your training is vitally important to your survival. You never can tell when you will need it. Now, pay attention, children. Nick, Niles, Jamie, Samantha!"

"Yes, Mr. Gabriels," they said in unison.

She ran down to the pantry, opened the secured door and walked over to the stereo. She put on her favorite music and began to stretch. The music changed and Sam began her workout, going through the routine her father taught her. Ever since she was five, her father brought her and her friends to this room. She had asked her father why they were training once. The only answer he gave was he wanted her to be prepared. The inevitable question always came next. At the age of ten she asked her father again, "Why are we preparing, daddy?"

He sat her down, thought for a long time, then simply said, "A time will come and our world will change." That was all he said and they continued their workout. As the years wore on, he continued shifting their training to include evasive maneuvers, weapons, and recon, just like soldiers trained for.

Sam finished her workout and was about to leave the house when her mom appeared. "Bye mom, see you later today."

"Wait, Sam. Who are you hanging out with today?" Sam's mother stopped her by the front door. Annie Gabriels was shorter than her daughter, with cropped hair black as coal, and streaks of gray that added character. Her face belied her age. She looked young and beautiful, with slightly slanted eyes in a green to match her daughters.

"Just the usual crowd. Niles, Nick, Jamie—and I think Mattie is coming too." Sam saw the expression on her mothers face, and she gave her a reassuring hug. "Don't worry mom, I won't get into too much trouble." With another hug her mom pushed her out the door. Sam's mother, Annie, had known Nick, Niles, and Jamie since birth. The foursome were all born within hours of each other and had been friends ever since. Their parents had agreed it was a sign of things to come. They encouraged their friendship, especially after Jamie's mother had to leave.

Annie knew only a little about Mattie Grant, since she had just arrived in Luella a year ago. Aron tried to find information, and eventually did. It showed her parents were separated, and she was currently living alone. She was attending school on a scholarship, was majoring in fine arts, and was very talented.

Standing in the shadows was the operative Aron had hired. He wondered what her plans were for the day and if she'd stick to routine and meet her friends. *This won't be easy. She's sneaky,* he thought. He almost lost her twice yesterday. Sam's father had taught her to evade and blend in with the crowds. With her father's departure the night before, he had no choice but to involve her.

Sam rushed out to the pod station and waited impatiently. She was headed to the central mall, where most of the stores and restaurants were located. She loved the Pizza Plaza; they had dancing, videos, and full size holo-rooms. Some of the hangouts had the cheap small ones, not the spacious rooms the Pizza Plaza supplied. Sam and her friends meet there every Saturday for some shopping, to exchange music and to do some dancing. Nick would create a new adventure program each week—rock climbing, car racing, beaches with white sand and light breezes—the stuff of dreams. Nick had this special bond with computers that defied description.

Sam looked up to see the tattered young man. He quickly looked away. The young man acted like he didn't see her. She knew otherwise and smiled to herself. As they got on the pod she glanced at him and said, "Hello."

He only responded by nodding then moving away. Sam grinned and wondered why he was so interested in her. Maybe her father left him to protect her? Sam was anxious as pod pulled into the main station. She was excited to meet her friends for the day. She curiously looked around and didn't see where the tattered young man had gone. If he was trying to be discreet, it was working. It would be just like her dad to leave a security detail in place.

Standing out of her line of sight, the young man thought. *Why did she have to be so pretty and aggressive?* Today she wore a mini-skirt, a pink tank top and black boots that reached almost to her knees. The outfit she wore should be classified as illegal. He never expected her to acknowledge him, let alone say hello. He knew he was in deep trouble here. He blended into the crowd and settled to wait and watch.

Sam shrugged off the tingling feeling, and headed toward Pizza Plaza. As she walked closer, she saw her friends Jamie Hutchins and Mattie Grant, followed not to far behind them were Nick and Niles, the McGovens twins. They were completely identical and boasted the same reddish brown hair, smoky gray eyes, and height. The only difference wasn't noticeable; Niles had been injured at the age of three. A piece of pipe had pierced just below his left collar bone and left a horseshoe shaped scar. Sam had little memory of that day, but she'd never forget the blood and screams. A shiver ran down her spine at the faint memory.

They reached the pizza shop and the twins headed to the counter to set up the holo-room for the group. Not far behind, the young man kept to the shadows. He looked twice when he saw the mouse brown hair. Was that who he thought? He wondered if Sam knew. She was smart and would figure it out soon enough. Her appearance would make his job harder. How could he reach Sam without that cell member noticing?

He couldn't risk his intelligence getting in the wrong hands. He'd just have to be patient and he hated that. Aron needed this information today. He took a seat on a park bench and scanned the crowd for other cell member flunkies.

Nick wandered back toward the group and said, "I hope you like this one. It took me over a week to make." Nick McGovens was a world-class computer genius, but sometimes he got ahead of himself. The last time they were here he developed a new car racing game, but in the last lap all the cars fell apart so no one won. Sam admired his creativity, charm, and fun nature. He also made her laugh, even when she was at her lowest.

A few minutes went by and then the door buzzed, popped open, and they walked inside. The sun appeared bright and warm. Parrots called out, tall palm trees stretched toward the sky, and white sandy beaches seemed to go for miles. The water was a clear light blue and you smelled the sweetness of the wind. Sam was in awe of the beauty and thought Nick had really out done himself. A parrot resplendent in a rainbow of colors, landed on a low branch nearby.

"Hope you got your bathing suit and sun screen?"

The waitress giggled when she entered. "Wow! You out did yourself Nick, but hey, you forgot the table. I'll have them get one and bring it in."

The gang just laughed. Nick blushed and fell over laughing at his mistake, kicking up sand. "I can't believe I forgot the table."

The girls went into the dressing room to put on their swimsuits. They commented that he should have programmed some more games. They liked the mystery game and the race game, but they couldn't dispute their love of the beach.

Niles and Nick were talking about what they'd heard, and how he'd been killed. Their dad, the chief of police, said that the only witness had been locked up for screening and physic interrogation from a Plutonus Military Intel officer. "Dad said this guy coming in was scary. The people he scanned weren't the same after." Sam shivered and ran her hands down her arms.

"Why would they bring in someone from Plutonus?" Sam asked.

The twins both smiled and answered, "We heard the witness

couldn't remember what happened or who killed the governor. That when they found the witness, he or she was still talking to the governor as if he was still sitting right next to them."

At that point Mattie splashed them. "Surf's up. The pizza will be done in like an hour, let's play."

Sam boomed away, as her thin sleek body sliced into the water she sprayed everyone on the side of the beach. Niles watched Sam and couldn't take his eyes off her long red hair, gleaming emerald eyes, and bikini-clad body. With a big grin, the twins glanced at each other, and off they went with a wild wave and doused everyone.

After a while, the waitress arrived with their pizza and drinks. The gang gathered around the table, ate, and talked about a few songs they liked. They made plans to go to the upcoming Phoenix Concert.

Jamie said, "Hey, I need a new set of earrings to match the outfit I just bought." At that, the girls started to get frenzied about shopping and Nick and Niles just shook their heads.

Robert Michaels watched from the dark corner of the Pizza Plaza, and had moved inside when Sam hadn't come out after an hour. There she finally was. He thought they'd never leave that holo-suite. Of course, she'd look even better than when she went in. Now he had to follow her and find a good spot to pass his information. He'd have to get a secure message to her father Aron there were very few he could trust now. She had to be one.

Later that afternoon, a few shopping bags heavier, Sam and Mattie walked and laughed. They headed toward the new boutique with the light blue outfit that Mattie loved. She'd been saving for months and could finally afford it. "You know, if that outfit was in a dark green, I'd buy it," Sam said.

"If I had your olive skin, I would too. I could stand a green, but with this light skin I have to stick to blue," Mattie snapped back.

Jamie walked up and laughed. "But I'm stuck with this copper skin, so I loved it in dark green, too. They only carry it in blue, yellow, and brown and I look awful in those colors."

Perfect. A crowded store. He would just slip in behind her—leave it to a girl to go shopping. Robert scanned the crowd and saw he'd been followed. *Time for a wardrobe change,* he thought. This look bothered him anyway. He looked a little too much like his cousin who was a cop.

Sam turned the rack and admired a pair of dark green pants. She felt his presence before he approached her. He whispered in her ear, "Shh. Here take this. Give it only to your father." He put light pressure on her arm and she felt a pinch.

Sam startled, took the data disk he'd passed her and stuffed it in her pocket. "Who are you?" She kept her eyes downcast and tried not to draw attention, like her father had taught her. It was too late. The tattered young man had taken off like lighting, and hadn't even glanced back. As he dashed, she noted that others had started to follow him. She shuttered and rubbed her arm. Why had this disk been so important?

Sam calmly walked over to her friends as to not draw attention. "I have to go. I forgot to do something that I was asked to do." She looked around trying to catch another glimpse of the man.

Mattie inquired frowned and glanced at her watch. "Why it's just afternoon. It's not even 4:00 p.m. yet!"

Sam snapped back around. "I forgot to do something my father told me to do."

Niles watched the play between Mattie and Sam. He had

become concerned with Sam's agitated state. Mattie had always trailed after them, watched Sam's every move. Niles decided he'd have to talk with her and find out what was really wrong. Right now, Sam had first priority. "We don't want to feel your father's wrath, so you better get going. We'll walk you to the pod station." She had acted strangely since she'd arrived at the plaza. If he thought she would have agreed, he would've taken her home personally. What had happened? What had changed?

"Hey, I'll just go with you. I can check in on my grandfather. I don't get to see him to often. He'll be happy to see me," Mattie said.

Niles sensed something had happened. He assessed Mattie and was determined to keep an eye on the situation. Sam's expression had turned distraught and she wasn't behaving like herself. She kept rubbing her arm. Why? Now, he knew something had changed.

Sam said, "Thank you." She paid for her earrings and pants, the whole time she searched the crowd.

It worked out well, a minute longer and he'd have been caught. Robert saw she'd left the boutique, but that cell member tagged along. He moved with a group of citizens that headed for the station.

The gang reached the pod station chatting about the latest new rock group. Ever observant, Sam noticed one of the men that had chased the young man. *Who could that young man be and why were they after him?* she wondered. *Would it have anything to do with the governor or possibly her father's trip?*

The tattered young man quickly ducked into a shop, and one of the men that had followed him ran past. Sam and Mattie got on, waved good-bye to the twins and Jamie promised to call.

When the pod streamed out of the station, Sam glimpsed a passer-by that had long black hair, and was well dressed. He waved at her with a smile. She wondered if that was the young man who'd been chased, but he looked somewhat familiar. She'd think about it later. She needed to get home and hand the disk to her father.

Robert couldn't help but smile at her. He had to remain focused and remember that he'd been followed. Now that he'd tagged her, it would be easier to keep track of her movements wherever she went. He headed home, loaded the tracking code, and caught some sleep. She wouldn't go far now. He'd catch up to his cousin and exchange news. The two males with Sam looked a lot like the chief of police.

As Mattie and Sam rode the pod Sam inquired, "I didn't know you had family on my side of town. They live so far from you." Since Sam met Mattie she'd a few suspicions. She showed up a year ago at the training center and just sort of planted herself in their group. Mattie had constantly called or sketched pictures of them or places they went. One day when Sam arrived home, Mattie was already there casually talking with her mom.

Mattie hesitated then answered. "Well, my grandfather moved there because he didn't want to move into a retirement center." Sam had no idea what to make of that answer and passed it off as nothing. A lot of people moved, some more than others, and she couldn't blame him for not wanting to be in an old folks home.

The pod reached Sam's stop she said, "See you later Mattie. Have a nice visit." She went left as Mattie went right. On the walk home, Sam contemplated what had to be on the disk and if her father had returned home yet. The hairs on the back of her neck prickled and she glanced back, but no one seemed to be there.

Sam wandered into the kitchen in search of a snack where her mom was finishing dinner. "Mom, is Dad home yet?"

"Well, it's only been a day," her mom said, giggling at Sam's reaction. "He'll be home in a few days, remember? He told you." Her mom kissed her on the forehead in a sign of reassurance, and Sam headed off to her room. She called her father to tell him of the encounter and of the disk. When he answered, he cut the call short. She'd heard a woman's voice in the background.

Sam was puzzled. Her father would usually say he loved her and would call right back. She paced her room and thought about the information on the disk. She tapped it against her leg. Why had he given this to her? She held the disk up and paced the small room some more. Sam finally reached the conclusion her father was headed into trouble and the disk would be of vital importance to the alliance. She called the only people that she trusted.

CHAPTER 4

AT FOUR o'clock, Aron Gabriels had entered the lobby across the street from the Hotel Dirtron and his phone rung. His daughter called and he didn't have time to speak to her, Ms. Weston approached hand extended. He answered made a brief comment and hung up. He noticed she wasn't alone and a man he didn't know followed close behind. She introduced him, Barnabas Matthew he said, and they shook hands. They proceeded to a conference room near her office on the fifth floor.

How can I help you, Ms. Weston?" he asked, concerned when he caught sight of the dark circles under her eyes.

With a weary sigh she said, "I've had a feeling the Governor was hiding information from me. There were many times when I couldn't reach him."

"Have you checked his day planner? Maybe he forgot to tell you." He reached over and patted her hand in a comforting gesture.

"I've checked. You need to understand, Mr. Gabriels. The governor and I were very close," She'd begun to cry and he handed her his handkerchief. Aron shocked by what she meant, sat there silently. He knew the governor had been very devoted to his wife. He couldn't believe and didn't want to believe what he'd just heard. His phone rang again. He saw Sam's name, answered, and hung up. He wasn't completely sure Lynn Weston told the truth. Something in her voice hadn't sounded right.

"What does Mr. Matthew have to do with all this?" He turned his head and looked at him as he stood near the door like a guard, arms folded across his broad chest.

"I'm here because of the numerous government transports that have been intercepted. We feel the governor was in charge of a rebel group called the alliance," Aron's eyes had widened in shock—the cell had killed his friend.

"That's not possible!" Aron shouted. He wanted to say more, but then remembered what he'd told the others.

She handed Aron a few invoices for explosives. "I found these invoices in his office when I was looking for his day planner."

"What do plan to do about this?" Aron asked. He took the papers and looked through them. A number of the invoices were for explosives.

"That's why I called you. These papers alone would ruin his family, if the information were to leak," Lynn said in a timid voice.

"Keep this quiet for now. I'll call you tomorrow." Aron pushed away from the table, his mind on the consequences. What had gone wrong?

Mr. Mathew and Ms. Weston stood up and joined him at the door. "We'll walk you out, mayor."

They kept close behind him, whispering in heated voices.

Sam three-way called Jamie, Nick, and Niles. "Can you guys come over as soon as possible?"

"Sure. What's up?" Nick asked.

"I'll explain everything when you get here," Sam replied with a sigh. She fingered the disk that lay on her desk.

"We'll be there before you know it. I'll bring my travel bag just in case," Jamie said.

While Sam waited on them, she tried to find out what was on the disk. She should have waited for Nick, but against her better judgment Sam ran the decoding program she had obtained from him. His program took a while to decode every file, and she hadn't realized how time had become her enemy. With in a few minutes, files opened. The same names, dates, and places kept showing up. She wrote them down in hopes of having information to pass to her friends.

Name	*Place*	*Time*
Lynn	*Dirtron Hotel*	*1:00 room 140*
Francis	*Dirtron Hotel*	*1:00 room 140*
Hilary	*Dirtron Hotel*	*12:45 room 140*
Barnabas	*Dirtron Hotel*	*1:00 room 140*

She pondered why they went to that hotel and who they were. Sam made a decision that this information was valuable and until she figured the rest, she'd make a copy and hide it. She taped one to the bottom of her dresser drawer and thought it would be safe, but now hide the original. She climbed on the chair, opened the air vent and taped it to the right hand side of the vent wall. "If they want to find it, they'll have to tear the house down," Sam giggled out loud. She'd used that hiding place on a number of occasions. Hidden deep inside were a number of articles, rings, disk, and credentials. She'd always dreamed of traveling beyond Pretoria. She had the strangest notion that that day would arrive soon.

After she'd cleaned up and hid any evidence of the disk, her mother shouted, "Sam, your friends are here to see you."

"Send them up!" she yelled down and walked to the window with that feeling again that she'd been watched. She pulled the curtains tightly shut.

"Okay, what's going on? We're here now, so spill," Jamie demanded with her usual candor as she ran a hand through her long blonde hair. Niles, always the logical one, wanted to know what they could do to help.

She told them about the tattered young man, what happened at the boutique, and how he'd been chased by as many as five other people. She left out the part about why her father had been involved and what role he played. Later, she would tell them everything. "And one of them may be hiding across the street." She looked nervously toward the curtained window.

Niles laughed out loud. "No way! We just walked past that spot." Curiosity got the better of him, and he peaked out the window and turned to the others in shocked disbelief. "I see someone, but he or she is hiding in the shadows. I can't make out the face or clothes."

"Where's the disk? I want to take a look around." Nick riffled through Sam's computer desk and with obvious delight he rubbed his hands together eager to crack the code.

"I hid the disk, but I have the information we my need to start with. I used that program you gave me last month. But I only had time to decode part of the disk."

As Sam told them about the information she read on the disk, the twins looked at each other and said at the same time, "That's the hotel where the governor was killed in Mantis." The twins blankly stared in astonishment at her.

Jamie sneaked a peek out the window. "I see the person hiding out there still. How are we going to get out of here? If he or she is watching from outside, maybe they've been inside. We need to get to a secure location and quickly."

"Hey, this is my job," Nick grabbed the phone and called his dad, the Chief of Luella Police Department. "Father, hey, there's a weird person hiding near Sam's house and we're all afraid to leave." Nick had given his code word to his dad to let him know there was really trouble. Nick and Niles never called him 'father' unless it meant trouble.

His dad replied with a touch of curiosity, "You usually don't call unless it's serious. I'll send some men out. Wait till they get there to leave. Okay Nick, see you when you get home and I'll expect an explanation."

Nick smiled and rubbed his hands together. "All set. After we watch the excitement, let's meet at the sandwich shop near the west end pod station. I'm getting hungry."

Sam grabbed the disk from under her desk drawer and her travel bag. Her father taught her to be prepared. The bag had always been packed with needed essentials like clothes, snacks, identification, and emergency debt sticks. When the group reached the foyer, they could see the police moving down the street looking for the stranger. They hotfooted in the opposite direction after the police went by and a slim figure dashed from the shadows.

Sam shouted, "If we get separated meet at the north pod station!"

CHAPTER 5

WHEN THEY reached the sandwich shop they sat and ordered a drink. Only then did they discuss who the people were on the list. Silence descended as the waitress took their order. When she left they started to talk again. They would have to be careful who heard them from now on. Nick hacked into the hotels data files doing a search to narrow down the possible suspects. Then Jamie called the hotel to see if any of them were currently staying there.

While Nick searched, Sam looked at her notes and called her father again. "I'm sorry Sam, I can't talk right now." Just like last time he answered and cut the call off abruptly. Sam felt troubled, what had her father gotten into and how much trouble could he be in? She looked to Jamie who in the past had lightened her mood.

Jamie reached over to her sensed her discomfort and gave her a hug. "Don't worry. We'll help him and you have the twins and me on your side."

"Got it," Nick exclaimed and pulled up a page showing all the names at Dirtron, except one, Hilary's.

Niles stared curiously at the page. "That can't be right; the rooms are wrong."

"Yes, but the governor had room 140, and they rented the rooms all around him."

"I wonder if they're still there." Sam pondered their next move.

With her father unreachable, who could they trust? In a flash, Detective Kane Michaels' name came to mind. How could she explain about her father's involvement with the alliance? He always said they could call if they were in trouble. After finding them at the McGovens farm, Detective Michaels had made a point of talking to them and finding out their plans. One night, he'd made a promise if they ever needed help he would be there, no questions asked. He'd even made them give up their fall back location, with reluctance. Sam thought for a moment then decided it would be best to wait. Things hadn't become that dangerous—yet.

"Wonder if they had anything to do with his murder?" Jamie tapped a finger to her chin.

"It shows they checked out, but I'm still searching," Nick told them and tapped away at his portable computer.

All of a sudden Sam felt they were being watched. The person stayed back in the shadows trying to be out of sight. Sam wrote a note to Jamie. Don't look right out the window, but there is a shadow near the ally just over my left shoulder. Jamie passed the note around the table to the others. She contemplated the idea of going to Mantis. Why not go to the source of the problem? Her father always told her that's where the best answers are found. Keep your enemies close if not closer. Sam wrote another note. Let's go to the pod station we need to take a long ride, if any one gets on we jump off.

"Give me one second to download the registration files to search through on the way." With a few keystrokes he was ready. His computer had to be near a wireless Internet source to work properly. He'd complained just last week when he saw the newest models to go on the market.

Sam impatiently waited for Nick's signal and kept her eyes on the street. Nick gave the signal and she checked out the window. "Everyone ready? Let's go, it's time for a road trip."

In a small apartment in Luella's center, a compact computer started beeping, alerting Robert Michaels that Sam was on the move again. Everything indicated she was headed out of town. Something had happened, This wasn't her normal Saturday routine. He rubbed the sleep from his eyes, picked up the device, and headed out. Before he left he gathered supplies, the latest in computer technology, and a few discreet weapons. As he slammed the door shut, he thought so much for sleep.

On his way down to the lobby, Aron called Sam back. He was curious to hear what was so important that it couldn't wait till he got back tonight. She had already called twice, so he thought that it must be critical.

Sam and her friends reached the station platform and impatiently waited on a pod to Mantis. Sam's phone rang light music. "It's my dad," She grabbed her phone, quickly answering. "Dad, what's going on? Why did you hang up earlier?"

Her father answered in a low voice. "Sam something has happened here in Mantis." He looked over his shoulder at the two figures following close behind, still in a heated discussion.

"Yes, I heard. What do you know of the murder about the governor of Mantis?" she asked impatiently.

"Only that it was a radical rebel group. We're trying to get in contact with our inside man now to confirm." Aron looked over his shoulder. Mr. Mathew had been paying close attention since he'd called his daughter. He continued his conversation with Sam and attempted to hush his tones.

Sam nervously bit her lower lip and told her father with hesitation what had happened. "Dad, I think your operative got in touch with me this afternoon."

Her father sensed her hesitation and lowered his voice. "Sam, where are you? Are you safe?" Aron Gabriels wondered what had he gotten his daughter into. They reached the lobby and headed left down a narrow corridor with Ms. Weston leading.

"Yes, I'm safe. Some friends and I are working on it. Yes, we are safe."

"Who is with you? What have you told them? What exactly are you working on?" He chuckled and knew his daughter and her friends all to well. He already had gray hair from their misadventures. Sam and her friends had kept him and Sam's mother on their toes. With them graduating soon it would be harder to keep track of them. Chief McGovens had the similar problems with the twins and they often took turns locating them.

Sam sounding timid said, "Just Jamie and the McGovens twins, Nick and Niles. Dad a young man gave me a funny disk. We're currently being followed and are changing locations."

"A disk! You looked at it didn't you? What was on it? What did it say? Where is the disk now?" Aron didn't realize Mr. Mathew had moved up behind him. He struck the back of Aron's head with the butt of his pistol. The phone dropped to the floor and his body followed.

"Yes, I looked. The disk is safe, I hid it and I have what I think you might need." The phone dropped to a fast beep and lost connection. Sam stared at the phone in awe.

Robert reached Sam's location as they boarded the pods for Mantis. He couldn't have cut it any closer, he saw she had chosen her friends better this time. He hopped on board the pod close behind her and moved to the snack car. He checked his watch, pulled out a compact computer, and walked over to wait on Sam's arrival. He held the latest hand held system he'd swiped from R and D after Aron approached him. *Let's see what she can do with this piece of equipment*, he thought.

He'd been undercover too long and his superiors were nervous. Their original suspect had been cleared years ago and even helped him head in the right direction. The frequency of sabotages had increased over the last couple of months and the number of missing cargo transports increased beyond understanding.

Sam sat there worried about what had happened to cause her to lose connection with her father. They decided to grab a bite to eat in the snack car; Nick missed out on his sandwich back in Luella and whined about his need to eat. It would be a long hour's ride on the pod to Mantis and no one wanted to hear him complain anymore. Niles went over the data and looked for matches. He'd always been good with statistics, and if he couldn't figure it out no one could. "Hey, look at the dates here on the sheet."

"They match all the unsolved murders that dad said they had a big task force trying to solve," Nick sounded excited at the prospect.

"But look, there is more then what his sheet had. These are over five years old," Niles pointed at the screen then looked at Sam curiously. Why would this guy give information to her? Sam had some explaining to do; Niles knew she would speak up when the time was right.

As everyone looked at each other, they knew they had to find out who those people where. Sam sipped her drink, her hand shaking slightly. She pondered her father's call again, and the waitress walked over. "Here. Someone wanted me to give this to you." She handed Sam a sleek black personal computer.

"Who gave it to you?" Sam frowned and looked around the car not recognizing any faces.

The waitress replied, "Some young guy with black hair." She shrugged and walked away. Sam spilled her drink when she turned back around. She quickly grabbed a napkin, wiping her hand off.

Nick looked overjoyed. "Wow, that's like ten times what my compact is. This one is better then the government issue! High speed and wireless and no need to be near a connection hub so we can go anywhere."

Sam voiced her thought out loud. "We need to get a private room to work out of when we reach Mantis so no one can find us. Listen, I have an idea. Let's go to the Dirtron and work from there. They wouldn't look there for us. We'll be right in their playground." The rest agreed quickly with a nod.

The young man smiled to himself. He'd done the right thing—that boy had brains. He wasn't sure about the brother—he acted edgy and constantly stared at Sam. Who could blame him though? The other girl, she's called Jamie, the jury was still out. She had a flighty look about her. Her father had instructed him that if anything went wrong he had to contact his daughter. He explained she could hide him and would know what to do with any information he found. When Aron pulled out a photo of his young daughter and her equally young friends, he was baffled. Aron said they could be trusted and mentioned in an off hand manner, they would take care of one of their own. What the hell he meant by that, Robert had no idea.

CHAPTER 6

THEY LOOKED at a map for the fastest way to the Hotel Dirtron upon reaching Mantis. When Sam, Jamie, and the twins reached the hotel, Jamie registered the room with her debit stick. If anyone looked for Sam Gabriels, they wouldn't find her—they'd find Jamie Hutchins' name listed.

The room was decked out with two separate sleeping areas, a table, a couch, and small kitchen. Nick headed for the table and started transferring the information from his compact to the new one. He opened a window to enter the information and another popped open with a list of trusted people. On the list were only two names. Nick and Niles glared with wide eyes at the screen.

"Guys, this only has Sam's and her father's name listed as trusted people. There's a log here that's only a little over a month old," Nick stammered in disbelief.

"Mine? Why would my name be on that list?" Sam strode over to look. What had her dad told this operative about her?

"Hey, Niles, get the list from Sam. I'm going to start cross checking." Nick's excitement had grown with the thrill of the chase.

"Sam, why don't you and Jamie crash for while. Nick and I have our work cut out for us," Niles turned his concerned gray eyes toward Sam. He had a feeling it was going to be a long night.

"That sounds like a good idea, and then we can check out that room." Jamie wandered over to one of the beds and crashed.

"Deal. I'm beat!" Sam walked over to join Jamie and had a hard time sleeping. She dreamt of her father and the unknown young man. The three of them were fighting for their lives. They stood in the middle of a field surrounded by armed operatives. They moved in slow motion, and she watched her father fall to the ground. The momentum of the dream suddenly picked up. Everything moved rapidly and she couldn't reach her fallen father. In the end, Sam stood by the young man as the sky turned bright orange and a great gust of wind had blown past them. Sam, startled, awoke, her heart pounding and her blood racing. She shook off the disturbing dream and tried to fall back to sleep.

Well, they're smart. They registered under Jamie's name. They'll be safe temporarily. Uh, oh, Robert thought. How could she be here? He thought they'd left her in Luella. He'd just have to stand watch and see whom she met. He'd made sure the waitress was paid well and had given her a message. She had been told if anyone asked about the group to send them toward the capital building. He'd bet he wasn't the only one to follow them.

When Jamie and Sam had woken up, hours had passed. Nick and Niles were still hard at work on the computer files and the list. Sam and Jamie took a walk to room 140 and grew more accustomed to the hotel—her dad would've called it recon. They stopped in their tracks when they heard a very familiar voice. One voice sounded like an older lady, the other one like a teenager.

The older voice asked, "Did you find the pesky brats?" She sounded upset. "You had your orders to stay with her."

The teenage voice said, "No, I lost them when they left the pod station. It was hard to follow them from Sam's house with the police all over the block, let alone follow them here. I wish I could find out what that waitress gave her, but she said it was just a note to meet someone at the government center. I waited there for about an hour and they didn't show."

Sam and Jamie looked puzzled and turned around hastily. They arrived back in their room and mulled over whom they over heard in the hall. Sam paced while Jamie lay down and stared at the ceiling. "I'm not sure, but it really sounded like—" Jamie snapped off. "Mattie. It was Mattie."

While Nick checked the dates, times, and activities of the names listed, he hadn't been listening to the girls. "Mattie what?" Jamie told Nick and Niles what they'd heard in the hall near room 140. By the time she reached the end, the twins had identical looks of anger spread across their faces.

"They must still be in the hotel, if not in the same rooms. Okay, let's follow them. Mattie." Niles shook his head in disgust.

Sam whipped around and glared at Niles. She'd put her hands up in frustration. "No. Aren't you listening? They're looking for us!"

"Yes, but what if we called Mattie? Ask her to meet us at our house in two hours. Mattie will have to go to the pod station. We can then watch the elevators from the main door of the restaurant and see whom she left with and try to get pictures. We can then match names to faces with my facial recognition program," Nick said calmly.

"Okay, I see your point. I have my camera and we have a nice compact computer to use." Sam reached into her bag to pull out the camera, a pair of sunglasses, and a hat to cover her hair.

Jamie expressed her idea next. "According to the registration logs their regulars. We could ask the hotel waiters and waitresses if they know their names. Yes, that's perfect."

"Okay, I'm going to call and ask her to meet me at the sandwich shop near school. I can't believe we trusted her," Sam had reached her boiling point and needed an outlet.

Niles took the camera Sam offered. "I thought there was something funny about her. Ever since that first day a year ago, I've had my suspicions."

"Niles, your right. I used to get an unsettling feeling around her," Sam shivered at the thought. Niles walked over and gathered her close for a reassuring hug.

"Don't worry. We'll figure it out." He ran his hands down her arms in comfort and felt her tension. They finagled sweet seats in the restaurant where they could see the elevator and the main exit of the hotel. Sam went out to a phone near the pod station in case they traced the call. She would stay and watch. After Mattie and company left she planned to return to the room. First, Sam called the hotel restaurant so her friends knew her position. Then she placed her important call to Mattie.

Why is she going back to the pod station alone now? Where were her friends? Robert thought, observing Sam's calls to her friends and Mattie. *Getting Mattie back to Luella had been smart thinking on her part,* he thought.

Mattie stared down at her phone in disbelief and answered quickly. "Hello?"

"Hey, Mattie, I'm going to go for bite to eat. Want to come?" Sam asked.

Mattie looked at the older woman and smiled when she replied to Sam. "Why, I'd love to, Sam. Where are we eating?"

"The sandwich shop near school in two hours," Sam replied casually.

Mattie hung up and turned toward the older woman. "We hit pay dirt. Sam's headed to the sandwich shop in Luella."

"Let's get a move on. She better be there, Mattie." The older woman looked down at her with scorn.

"She will. Sam's not one to skip out," Mattie said with confidence.

Mattie walked down the hall near the front desk and Jamie started taking pictures. Niles, positioned outside, watched as they walked through the front door, down the street, and towards the station. Nick quickly downloaded the pictures and sent them to the printer at the front desk.

Robert couldn't believe his eyes as he focused in. There they stood on the platform, five cell members. Now, who were these other people with Mattie? Could this get any more complicated?

When Jamie picked up the photos from the front desk, the concierge asked curiously. "Why are you taking pictures of the assistant to the Governor of Mantis?"

Jamie flashed a sweet smile and blushed. "What picture is she in?" The concierge pointed her out. Jamie marked it, smiling again. "Thank you. Do you know any of the others?" She batted her eyelashes for effect and gained an even deeper blush from the concierge.

The concierge leaned on the desk, inching closer to her. "No, but I see them a lot. They come in regularly for lunch." He passed Jamie a card with his personal number on it that said, "Call me, please." Robert followed Sam back to the hotel. He had a bad feeling about the whole situation. He wanted to stick close by, and took his post across the street again. He scanned the hotel, located Sam and her friends, and settled back to listen.

Jamie hurried back to the room floating on cloud nine. "Sam, I found out one of the names from the front desk concierge. He told me without me asking and handed me his number. Drum roll please, she was the assistant to the governor. Her name is Lynn Weston. The others come in here all the time, but they don't stay here. He also said that only Ms. Weston stayed here on the night of the murder." Jamie held out the pictures with Mattie and Lynn Weston as they left the hotel.

Sam excitedly took the pictures from Jamie and thumbed through them. She laid the pictures on the center of the table and stared down at them. "One down, three to go. Nick, what are you working on?" She peaked over his shoulder to look at the monitor.

"I'm getting all of the calls from Ms. Weston's room and searching for her mobile cell service provider." As Nick studied the screen of the compact he gasped. There were three or four calls a day to Mattie.

Sam thought the pod would be half way to Luella by now. With a grin on her face she glanced up at Jamie. "Let's play some mind games with Mattie."

"What are you thinking of?" Jamie watched Sam closely and grabbed her phone eagerly.

"We can play cat and mouse with her from here. We'll drag her everywhere with phone tag," Sam knew her friends would agree on this maneuver.

Niles, not one to be left out, wanted in on the action. "Hey, let me call and ask her to help me with my compact. I'll say Nick is at the station working with dad. Have her meet me at the library on the third floor."

Jamie snorted. "Oh, that's great! Then after you call, I'll give her about thirty minutes. I'll call and tell her I'm at the pizza shop at the north pod station terminal. I have another disk Sam gave me."

"Then I'll call. First, I have to try to call my dad again; if that doesn't work I can call some of his friends I know he trusted," Sam thought of Detective Michaels again and shook her head. Would he keep his promise not to tell the chief?

Niles thought of how pissed Mattie would be after all that running. "But how do we narrow who is who from the rest?"

"You call all the phone numbers that we don't recognize. They might say their names. If they ask why you're calling, say Ms. Weston wanted them to meet at the hotel and hang up. While you're on the phone, I'll see if we can get a location from a GPS or a trace source location on Mattie. We need to keep track of her location," Nick said and went back to work on the computer.

Sam called her father and impatiently waited for the ringing to stop. He finally answered in a low scratchy voice. "Sam, listen. You have to get hold of that operative that gave you that disk. Get help from Chief McGovens or Kane Michaels if you can't reach him. They have me in a building. You can try a GPS tracer, but I don't think it would work. I can barely get a phone signal. Now, I'm safe, but you need to expose them before they get the—" The phone went dead.

Sam looked astonished and determined. She sat on the couch clutching the phone in her hands. Fire blazed in her belly and she took charge. "Guys, the plan has changed. Nick, we need to call your father now and send what we know to his secured e-mail. Have him look at the files, but keep the pictures till later. Let's see if our young man can help us. I'm going to go outside. He's been trailing me the last couple of days, and I thought dad put him on security detail. My dad trusted him or I wouldn't be on the list. Jamie, watch me from the hotel restaurant."

The twins asked, "So, we're going to still play cat and mouse?"

"Still sounds likes fun to me and it'll buy us some time," Jamie moved back to the couch punched in Mattie's number.

Sam looked exasperated. "They have my dad locked up somewhere so we may have to do it a different way." Sam heard the collective sound of discontentment throughout the room.

"Sam, let me go with you. I don't think you should do this alone," Niles walked closer to her and took her by the hands. "We should stick together."

"No, I have to do this part by myself. Thanks for the offer," She removed her hands from his grip and edged toward the door. "If anything happens, take that disk and get it to Detective Michaels. He's not just a detective." With that she left the room. How much could she tell her friends without harming her father? All would be known soon.

CHAPTER 7

SAM WALKED out of the hotel and to the walkway with a determined stride. She pulled her cap down low and hunched her shoulders. She turned in a slow circle, scanned the crowd, and found the young man across the way. She recognized him only because of the artificially enhanced eye. Tonight he had dirty blond hair not black. Sam walked slowly toward him with confidence in every step. The young man smiled and slipped into an alley. Sam followed and checked her back.

When she entered the alley he grabbed her by the arm and pushed her up against the wall with his hard male body. To an observer it would look like two lovers who shared an intimate moment. "What are you doing?" he demanded. His cool blue eyes never left hers. He pushed closer and ran his hands quickly down her sides and back. He found a weapon in the small of her back and removed it.

For a minute Sam stood frozen and speechless. "They grabbed my dad and have him somewhere. We have their photos and know two of their names. One is Lynn Weston. My father told me to find you," She finally stammered after a moment or two.

"How do you know they have your father?" Robert questioned this was new information to him.

"After I tried contacting him a number of times today he finally answered. He said he was being held." Sam answered slightly out of breath as he searched every part of her.

"How do I know you're telling me the truth?" Robert pocketed the weapon and slowly moved down her legs, finding the knife she kept in her boot.

"You'll just have to trust me." Sam smiled up at him now that he was standing the top of her head just reached his chin.

"Well, I only know them by number; names weren't important. You have me at a disadvantage." He'd given her that trademark smile, the one she'd seen on the platform.

Sam's stomach flipped again and she resisted the urge to put a hand to it. She had been trapped by two steel bands, and she could feel every muscle in his broad chest. "Good. Then you can help us. We have our own network of trusted people."

"Okay, but we better be careful. They've killed agents who have tried to get close. Let's take a look at what you've got, and then make some calls. Gather our troops together and make it work." Sam had him in her web before she'd even spoken. She smelled of strawberries and looked just as delicious. The picture he had of her didn't do her justice.

Sam cocked her head and looked up at him. The question that burned at the back of her tongue came out. "By the way, what's your name?" He'd given a low throaty growl as she ran her tongue over her lips.

"It's Robert." He released her reluctantly as they stepped cautiously out of the alley. The whole time he monitored the crowd and made sure they weren't followed. He wrapped an arm around her waist, pulled her close, and hurried her across to the hotel. They entered through a side entrance that led to a stairwell.

Robert questioned what he had done. He couldn't possible help her; he'd risked exposing himself and her father. He grimaced.

Robert could never resist a red head in distress, and that seemed to be his one flaw in life.

Sam took him to the room and introduced him to the others. She showed him the pictures they'd spread out on the table, and filled him on what they knew. He wrote what he knew on each of the photos then handed them back to Sam. She took the pictures over to Nick for scanning. "Now, where do you think they might have my father?" she asked, taking command again.

It was a new experience for him. He used to be in command of his own unit, and taking orders was not one of his strong points. For now he'd let her feel like she was in charge. The guys in his unit would've had a field day if they'd found out he, their colonel, had been led by a woman. He sighed. "Well, they have two or three safe houses they use in town." He started to locate all the safe houses in the area and marked them for the twins on a map. The twins looked up the call to Aron's phone. Nick had set up a long e-mail, tracked it, and triangulated the phones current position. Glancing at her watch, Sam decided they would continue their game. Mattie would reach Luella shortly.

Jamie called Mattie at Sam's command. "Hey, Mattie. I'm at the computer department library. You want to go to the holo-room and swim? I have the program that Nick did, but with a table."

"I'm on my way to meet Sam at the sandwich shop." Mattie turned away from Ms. Weston with a frown. "Last I heard Sam was working on some disk she found at the computer department and hasn't left there yet." Sam scribbled a note down trying to think of what to do if Mattie refused to play along.

Mattie sighed and said, "Okay. I can come meet you. We can pick up Sam too."

Jamie informed Mattie that she'd wait at the far top end of the building away from the computer department. "I'm on my way. See you soon." Jamie had given them a smile and thumbs up as she returned the phone to her purse.

"Well, what's going on? Where's Sam?" Lynn Weston demanded an answer and Mattie flinched. Mattie wanted to make things right or her situation would be in grave danger. She'd lose her scholarship, her apartment, and her dignity.

"She's at the computer department. That was Jamie, she said Sam found a disk. I'm to meet Jamie at the department library." Mattie felt sick to her stomach and swallowed hard. Maybe she'd find Sam first and get back in Lynn's good graces.

"We'll split up. You go meet this Jamie. The rest of us will go take care of Sam and that disk. We can't let that operative get to her." They reached Luella and changed course for the computer department.

Aron had been trying to figure out where they'd left him. From where he'd sat there were no doors, windows, or vents. The last thing he remembered was coming down a long hall while he talked to Sam. Ms. Weston and Mr. Mathew were escorting him out. The next thing he knew, someone hit him from behind and he blacked out. He wanted to know what was going on and who'd hit him. The room looked like an ordinary conference room. He didn't notice the e-mail his phone received.

"I got it, but it can't be right," Nick said. He frowned, rechecked his data, and scratched his head.

"What do you mean?" Sam stopped pacing. It wasn't like Nick to be wrong.

"He's right across the street—a thousand feet away—unless

he's behind the building," Nick looked puzzled and scratched his head again.

"Is there any meeting areas close by?" Sam looked at Robert.

"Whenever I met with them it was outside the water tower behind the building. I've never been to any of the safe houses." He started to pace the room rubbed his chin in thought. What could he be missing? He'd met them a number of times in that exact location. Could he be wrong about the location? Is it possible the signal was being reflected off another source in case anyone looked for Aron? "Nick, walk around the building see if you can get a better signal."

Sam started to pace in the opposite direction of Robert while deep in thought. Where could they be holding her father and we're so close? she thought. She turned and looked out the hotel window. The sun had begun setting lower in the sky; Robert quickly joined her and pulled her away. "Don't stand there! The city has eyes." He drew the drapes closed and continued to pace.

How could he go there undetected? They knew he hadn't been completely honest with them. Now they had gone too far. No one was supposed to get kidnapped. They'd gone too far when they killed the provincial governor. The cells' standard practice had been deviated from. Why? They took out their targets; they didn't hold them. What's going on? What changed? Aron had been Robert's last hope. Now he'd have to deal with a bunch of misfits who seemed determined to rescue her father and everything else be damned. He had to be nuts to stay and help them, but what choice did he have? He had to complete his mission, no matter what. Robert had orders direct from the top.

CHAPTER 8

In Luella, Chief Patrick McGovens received the data Nick sent. *"What is all this data and what have these boys gotten themselves into now?"* he thought. He got up and locked the door to his office and started reviewing the data. He opened the file and studied it intently until he came across names from unsolved cases. Nick had also included the list of trusted people. The chief decided to call in one of his most trusted detectives, Kane Michaels.

He picked up the phone and dialed his extension. "Detective Michaels, can you come in my office for a minute?" Whatever his sons were involved in this time it was major. First the code word now this secure e-mail.

"Sure, Chief." A few minutes later there was a knock on the door and Patrick opened it. In swaggered Detective Michaels. He was a young detective, but was a straight shooter, not one likely to take a bribe. Kane was fast becoming a confidante to him and his sons. Kane had taken to his boys right off, forming a lasting friendship. The year before he proved how valuable he was to the department. He was sent on a mission to find the twins. When they didn't want to be found, they were hard to track. A certain blond haired, blue-eyed young lady had caught his eye. He smiled, remembering their first encounter.

"Have a seat." The chief relocked the door and sat back down.

His sons were going to make him completely gray before his time.

"What did you need to see me about?" Detective Michaels inquired, noticing the chief's troubled expression.

"We have a situation that needs immediate attention, but it has to be done quietly. The mayor of Luella has been kidnapped and I've received data that incriminates a government official."

"Where did this data come from?" the detective asked. The chief visibly stiffened then laughed.

"Well, how do I put this?" The chief blushed and started rubbing his hands together in a nervous manner.

By the look on the chief's face, Kane Michaels knew the answer already. "Don't tell me your sons are involved and the others too?"

"What's new? When aren't they involved?" He turned his monitor around so that Michaels could take a look.

"Is that what I think it is?" He was staring at the monitor with a look of impending doom. "Dates, times, missing persons, unsolved cases . . . could this information implicate the alliance or another group?"

"Yes and more," the chief replied.

Running a hand through his black hair Kane asked, "What do you want me to do?" Military Intel would want to know of this untimely development. This is exactly the information they wanted him to look out for. How did the kids get a hold of it? He wondered.

"Let me check with the boys and see if there have been any developments."

"I can't believe we're doing this." Michaels ran his fingers through his hair again making his disheveled hair even messier.

The chief pulled up a blank e-mail and composed a message to the twins. He informed Kane of the events earlier in the day hoping it would make sense to someone.

Nick, I have Detective Michaels who I trust and was on your safe list. What is the current situation and have you located Sam's father? -Dad

Back in Mantis Nick's computer started beeping, breaking the tense atmosphere of the room. "What's going on now?" Robert wanted to know and looked to Nick.

"It's just an e-mail from our dad. He wants to know what the situation is and how to proceed." He gazed back to where Sam was sitting with Jamie.

"Who exactly is your father?" Robert inquired he had a feeling he already new and was almost afraid to ask.

"None other than the provincial Chief of Police," Nick cocked a grin at Robert in reply.

"I told you we had our own network. Now where do we go from here? Aren't you the expert?" Sam faced Robert, hands on her hips and face glowing. She turned the reins over to where they should've been from the beginning.

Not taking his eyes off Sam he answered. "Send him the pictures of the cell and let him know that you're playing phone tag. He'll be able to pick up Mattie and Ms. Weston at the location you have stated. Tell him we have the location of Sam's father. Whatever you do, don't let him know I'm here." Robert began to pace again. He'd had his suspicions confirmed about the twins, his cousin had mentioned them. He also needed distance from Sam. If he didn't have it, he might just grab her and show her how to network. *Boy, wouldn't that put Niles in his place,* he thought. He put a hand to his mouth to stifle a laugh.

Niles watched Robert pace as Nick relayed the information. He wondered what was with him and why he didn't want their dad to know he was here. Sam's starting to look worn out. Maybe he could get her to stop pacing for a while or Jamie could give her a calming tea, Niles thought. He felt like his hands were tied, and he wished there was more they could do than wait.

The chief's computer beeped and received Nick's message.

Dad- Attached you will find photos taken this evening at the Hotel Dirtron. Some are marked with Cell members' names or numbers as we know them. At least two of them are on their way to Luella's training center computer department. They should be there anytime we have been playing phone tag in order to buy us some time. Take only the officers you trust and were on the list. Dad, use that new imaging software I gave you to identify the others. Call Sam and Jamie's parents and give them some excuse, we're staying in Mantis for now. Thanks Dad.

"Here's our answer. Grab some officers from that list and let's roll. By my calculations, we don't have much time." He looked down at his watch noticing the time and holstered his weapon.

"I'm on it, chief." Detective Michaels left the office to gather the officers.

Chief McGovens and Detective Michaels, along with four other trusted officers, headed to the training centers computer department. They agreed it was best to use the element of surprise.

Mattie called Ms. Weston in a panic. "I'm where Jamie told me to meet her, but I don't see her. Could the operative have gotten to her?"

"We're still looking for Sam, but so far nothing. I thought you trusted her."

"I do. This isn't normal. I should have stayed closer." Panic gripped her. If she failed she'd never see the money to finish her education. Ms. Weston recruited her specifically. By doing her aunt this favor, Mattie was promised full tuition and room and board. All she had to do was stick close to Sam and her family, and then report back any unusual activity. She had a job waiting at the museum after graduation, even if it was just cataloging. Who knew where it would lead.

Just then, the chief arrived on the lower level and arranged the officers.

"Detective Michaels, take one officer with you to the third floor. Get Mattie Grant back to the station. I'll take the rest and get Lynn Weston. Remember, try to take them with little notice and get it done quickly."

Detective Michaels headed up to the third floor and spotted Mattie looking around. He'd met her on occasion at the Gabriels' home. He didn't trust her. Then, one day he found her alone snooping in Aron's den. He walked up behind her and grabbed her elbow. "Please, quietly move toward the elevator and don't say a word." Mattie tried to resist, but knew it was futile. The detective had a strong hold on her; there was no escape.

On the lower level, Ms. Weston had just finished giving the order to search the other levels. She scanned the crowd one more time and saw the officers. She started to back away, looking for a way out. When she turned around, there was the chief. "Hello, Ms. Weston. Nice evening for a walk."

Lynn looked infuriated. She stalked toward the exit with the chief and three officers on her heels. "I won't tell you anything." She tried to quicken her pace, and the officers closed ranks around her.

"It doesn't matter—we know enough. Let's go have a nice chat." He took her arm in a light grasp. Outside the training center she spotted the others and gave them a slight hand signal.

Aron Gabriels became dizzy and sat down at the table rubbing the lump on his head. What he wouldn't do to have a cup of Jamie's tea right now. He put his head in his hands to stop the room from spinning. That's when he noticed the e-mail from Nick. Excitement flared anew. "I knew I could count on Sam and her friends." Relief showed on his face. He hoped Robert had enough sense to keep an eye on Sam. She'd know how to contact him and he will keep her safe. Now, how was he going to get out of this room? Realizing that Sam could e-mail him, he sent off a message, giving her his last known position. He also wanted to know if Robert was there. He'd be able to get him out—not that his daughter couldn't. Today, he needed more experience and Robert was it.

Across the street at the hotel, Nick's phone beeped. There was an incoming message. Everyone just stopped and stared at Nick's phone. Sam leaped over the couch and grabbed the phone. "It's my father." Sam had a look of relief on her face.

"What's it say?" Robert tried to take the phone out of her hand, but with a glare from Sam he pulled away.

"His last meeting was at the building across the street at Lynn Weston's office yesterday at four o'clock. That was about the time I lost contact with him."

"I'll pull up the design plans so we can get a layout of the building." Nick quickly went to work.

"How do you plan to do that Nick?" Sam was curious about that look in his eye. She had seen that look before when he was mad at a classmate. He had falsified police records and put out a warrant for his arrest. He was definitely up to no good.

"Just the latest back door I found." Sam looked skeptical knowing his history. Chief McGovens would not be happy—he was breaking a number of laws. She smiled.

"Great. I'm dealing with a bunch of criminals." Robert plopped down on the bed.

Sam went over to him and gave her best smile. "Now do you believe me?" With her hands out to the side she walked back to Nick with that know it all wiggle.

"Okay, here we go." With a curious look on his face he pointed at the screen. "Niles does this plan look incomplete to you?"

"It sure does. I wonder where that leads to." He pointed to a hallway on the map following its path from start to finish. "That hallway just stops. There's no door."

Robert leaned over Nick's other shoulder to get a closer view and brushed Sam's arm. She quelled the shiver that ran down her body from the contact. It's probably nothing. Just her imagination, she thought.

"I have a suggestion. Pull up a map of the block. See what's close by." Nick did what Robert suggested. "Now try an overlay. Would you look at that. The water tower across the street connects to the building!"

With a look of determination, Sam straightened up. "How are we going to get into that building? It's not like we can walk through the lobby."

Niles smiled. "I have an idea. Nick, remember that security

program you wrote when you were ten?" Nick grinned and rubbed his hands together.

"Oh, brother." Jamie threw up her hands.

"Oh yes. I still have it. Comes in handy when I want to cut class."

"Wait," Robert put up a hand. "What does this program do?" Robert was still looking over the plans for the building. He looked up when Nick answered.

"Fire drill time," he said, and with a twinkle in his eye he pulled the program up and began setting the timer.

"We'll have to time it just right and sneak past the firemen. Niles, you seem to notice odd things. Make sure we have an exit strategy." He didn't like the idea of drawing attention to the building. Two men and two kids would draw more notice coming out of a dark alley especially if one was injured.

Sam turned around to gather her things. Niles noticed her agitated state he walked over. "I don't think this is a good idea. Sam, you have to stay here." Niles shared a look with Robert that said "back me up here." She continued to pull weapons from her bag, ignoring Niles.

"Sam, leave it to me to get your father out." Robert took a step toward her, but she didn't back down. With a look of determination in her eyes Sam took a step toward the door.

"There's no way I'm staying behind. I have the training to get him out." Sam locked eyes with Robert.

Robert saw this was not going to be easy. There was no time for a debate and he didn't want to baby-sit more than he had to. The less he took with him, the better his chances of success, no mater what her training. "Look, I'll take Nick and Niles with me.

Nick will be able to get me past any security and Niles seems to remember the layout pretty damn good." He moved to block her exit. "Besides we won't have much time to get in and out. I can get your father back here a lot quicker without you." The words were out of his mouth before he could recall them. He winced closing his eyes briefly.

Sam stared at him in disbelief. This man definitely didn't know her. She could take him down and he wouldn't know what hit him. She took another step toward the door and Robert.

"Sam, listen to him, he's right. Please just stay here." Niles grabbed her shoulders from behind, turned her around, and gave her a gentle shake. She saw genuine concern on Niles' face. With an oath, Sam gave in. If anyone else would've touched her, they would've found themselves flat on their backs.

Jamie and Nick watched the whole time. Jamie couldn't believe Sam had two gorgeous guys fighting to be her champion. It was just her luck that she couldn't get either one of them to notice her. Jamie felt a tap on the shoulder and turned to Nick. "Jamie, I'll show you what to push in order to set off the alarms." Nick pulled Jamie by the hand to the computer and showed her the program.

Nick, Niles, and Robert headed to the front of the hotel and waited for the firemen to arrive. Robert was surprised by the gear they had packed in their travel bags; he'd never met anyone like this foursome. They carried a small arsenal between the four of them, and from what he saw they knew how to use them.

CHAPTER 9

IN THE Luella Police Department interrogation room Mattie sat with her head in her hands, distressed. What could have gone wrong? Why was she there? That detective looked so much like that operative. How could that be? She'd seen him before, but where?

A deep gruff voice addressed Mattie. "Mattie Grant or is it Mattie Ulysis?"

Mattie's head swung up at the question. She was looking at a man that resembled the other and was in shock. With a note of fear in her voice she asked, "How do you know that?"

"First, I've seen you around Sam and at the Gabriels' home. Second, Sam and her true friends decoded a disk; your name came up in conversation. Third, after I caught you in Mr. Gabriels' den, I ran your prints. Now, the big question. What do you want with Sam and who are you working for?" Detective Michaels stared intently at Mattie waiting on her response.

"Don't you know? You seem to know my name." She crossed her arms over her chest in defiance.

"What I know is that you're working for the alliance, specifically in a cell intent on undoing all their accomplishments," Mattie looked at him with confusion on her face.

"What do you mean? I work for the government. Lynn Weston was the executive assistant to the governor and I work for her."

"So, what is your reason for following Sam?" Kane stood with his hands braced on the table, staring down at her.

"I was told Sam's father, Aron Gabriels, needed protection from a cell member and I was to report back to Aunt Lynn when he showed up." Detective Michaels was trying to determine if Mattie was telling the truth. He straitened and crossed his arms across his chest running a hand across his chin in contemplation.

"What do you know of this cell member who was trying to hurt the mayor?" She was staring at him and trying to figure out her answer—what she could tell him that he didn't already know.

With a befuddled look Mattie decided to answer honestly. "Well, he kind of looked like you, except he has an artificially enhanced eye, blond hair, and an identification tattoo on his left wrist."

He started laughing grabbed his stomach and flashed his own tattoo. "Well that sounds like someone I know and he's definitely not the bad guy." He quickly left the room to many curious stares. Mattie was left stunned by this discovery and couldn't believe her ears. He returned a moment later holding a picture frame, he pointed at the picture. "You were looking for him, correct?"

Kane was holding a picture of himself and Robert on their last mission. "That's him! How do you know him?" She took the picture from the detective to study it closer.

"Tell me everything you know about Lynn Weston and her associates. In return I'll tell you about my cousin." Mattie looked resigned, but told Detective Kane Michaels everything. On the other side of the mirror Chief Patrick McGovens smirked at the ease of Mattie's cooperation. She didn't seem the type to be working on the wrong side and usually his instincts were right. Kane was glad to see he wasn't wrong this time either.

A half hour later, Kane joined him. "Are we ready for Lynn Weston? She doesn't have any idea how much is actually going on or what real danger she was in. She was able to give us a few more names."

The streets of Mantis were filled with shadows. No one noticed the three shadowed figures blending in with the crowd. The local nightlife had just started to pick up and partygoers were meeting with friends. Loud music could be heard drifting from the clubs open doors and bright lights from the neon signs reflected an eerie glow across the sidewalk.

Out of the darkness a shrill noise pierced the air. The crowd from the nightclub filed out to see what was happening. More sirens approached and the noise level became deafening. The firemen converged on the building from all sides, opening entrances and exits.

"Isn't there someone up there?" Niles said to a girl in the crowd. She started screaming and pointed up. The three figures slipped through a side door during the commotion. Nick easily disarmed the alarm and keyless entry.

"Whew, that was close. Let's get moving. By the way, nice work Niles." Robert slapped Niles on the back. With more training they wouldn't be half bad. He could have used both their skills in the past.

"Well, I really thought I saw someone," he answered shyly moving toward the hall.

"Good work anyway. Which way do we go, Niles?"

"This is the fastest way." Niles led the way, avoiding the firemen. They reached the hall, but there was no visible door. Robert started scanning the walls trying to find a panel.

"Now what? I can't seem to find an entrance." His artificial eye couldn't penetrate through certain types of metal.

"You have to be patient, Robert. We'll just do it the old fashion way." They started tapping on the walls. Niles took one side and Nick took the other.

"Here it is! How clever. It blends in so well." Nick worked on breaking the code. He used his latest computer security program. To Robert it seemed like an eternity, but it was only a few seconds. He scanned the building, locating the firemen. He saw them working their way down from the top floors.

"Got it. That was a piece of cake." They heard a noise like an elevator and then the door opened. As they watched through the door, the floor began to appear, then the room. The mayor of Luella sat at the conference table, a stunned look on his face. He immediately moved to the side of the room in defensive mode until he realized who exactly was staring at him from the shadows.

"Holy cow! How did you ever find me?" He moved slowly toward them, fighting the dizziness and hanging onto the table edge.

"These troublesome kids! Look what they have done." With a slight grin, Robert walked over to the mayor and started escorting him out of the room. "We need to get a move on before the firemen make it to this hall."

"Okay, but where exactly am I?" He rubbed his forehead trying to steady himself.

"There will be time for answers later. We need to move." They proceeded out of the building, staying in the shadows. Niles noticed the office directory where government names were listed and stopped in his tracks, causing Nick to bump into him.

"What's wrong, Niles?" his brother was staring at the directory with a frown.

He then pointed to specific names on the board. "Take a look. Anything look familiar?"

"I can't believe this. We have to tell the others." They entered the alley behind Aron and Robert.

Robert focused on the safe house nearby and saw movement. A curtain slid to the side and a man's face appeared. "Get back in the club crowd, the alley is being watched," he commanded almost shouting to be heard over the noise.

"How long do we need to stay here?" Aron was leaning on the wall and had paled somewhat.

"Just a few minutes, Aron." Robert noticed the curtains close and hurried behind a group headed for the hotel. They entered through another side door and made it back to the room safely.

CHAPTER 10

SAM COULDN'T stop pacing and they had just left. "What is taking so long?" she asked herself.

Jamie was sitting at the computer and moved to the mini-bar. She picked a bottle at random and poured. "Would you stop pacing? Sit and drink this." She handed Sam a glass with amber liquid. If that didn't work, she'd mix up a calming tea for her.

Sam looked at the glass in her hand. "What is it?" She sniffed it and made a face.

Jamie swirled the amber liquid mesmerized by the color. "Not sure. I got it from the mini-bar."

Sam took a gulp of the liquid. With tears in her eyes, she choked out, "Boy, that burns."

Jamie took a sip of hers. "Feel better yet?"

Sam started pacing again. "No. Is there any more of that? I hate to drink alone. Join me in another." She held up another bottle waving it at Jamie.

"You're right. This does burn, but not like that batch Niles made last summer. Now, that was good stuff." In the background they could hear the fire truck sirens getting louder.

"Sam, what do you think about Robert?" Sam poured herself another drink and lined the bottle up with the others. She contemplated her answer for a minute.

"I'm not sure, but he sure is cute. God, have you looked into those intense blue eyes of his, not to mention all those muscles. I think I've seen him before." Jamie opened another bottle and refilled her glass.

"I've had that feeling too." They shared a look, burst out laughing, and raised their glasses in a toast.

"It's been at least twenty minutes. What's the hold up? I need another drink. Jamie, would you like another?" Sam swayed a little and held onto the counter.

"Sure, why not. How about Niles, Sam? You do know he worships the ground you walk on," she giggled.

"Yes," she said with a sigh, "but I don't like him in that way. He's more like a brother. I don't want to hurt his feelings." Sam noticed the forlorn look on Jamie's face.

"Now, how do I get Niles to notice me or any man for that matter?" Jamie groaned and flopped down on the bed.

"Quit trying so hard. Niles doesn't like girls to flaunt over him. He'll like you just because you are you. You're gorgeous. Trust me, they look."

Jamie raised her head and her voice. "How can you say that when you are so pretty even Robert can't keep his eyes off you? Now pass that bottle back." Sam blushed and turned away deep in thought. *Does he really notice me? How had she missed it?* she thought.

Just then, the door handle rattled and in walked Robert followed by Aron. The look on Sam's face was priceless. Aron said in his most commanding voice. "Oh, worried were we. Samantha, what do you think you're doing, young lady?"

"Dad!" Sam rushed past Robert and gave her dad a hug almost knocking him over.

"The least you could do, Sam, is offer your father a drink, too." He hugged Sam while taking in the state of the room. Photos, food containers, and a number of empty bottles littered the room.

Robert, Nick and Niles had scattered around the room looking on in astonishment. Niles took a look at Jamie in a new light. She was passed out on the bed with a bottle of rum cradled in her arms.

"Sam, how much have you had to drink?" Robert seemed concerned and walked over to the mini-bar, which was almost empty.

Sam giggled and said, "Just a little, I think." She walked away from her dad to lean against the table.

"I knew we should've emptied it before we left," Niles gave a low moan and remembered what happened when they drank the summer before. Jamie and Sam started to dance and were half undressed before she passed out. Detective Michaels arrived and took the situation in hand, making sure everyone made it home safely. He shook his head to clear the memory away.

"Niles, you're so cute when you shake your head like that." He blushed at her comment and walked Sam carefully to the other bed before she fell.

"Sam, it's time for you to get some sleep." She leaned her head on his shoulder and yawned.

"Wait," she put a hand to his chest, his heart rate picked up pace. "You do know you're my best friend and I could never date you, right?"

In a low voice Niles asked, "Do we have to discuss this now, Sam?"

She looked behind Niles and saw Robert watching them. Her eyes turned to sparkling emeralds. "No, Sam. Why?" Robert's stomach hit rock bottom when his gaze connected with hers. With a look of rejection Niles stared at Robert over his shoulder.

"He's just too sexy!" Sam blurted out. She slumped in Niles' arms and he placed her gently in bed and gave a kiss on her forehead.

"Sleep tight," he said.

The room was thick with male tension. Aron just shook his head and turned to Robert. "Now, what is going on and start from the beginning. Since Jamie's already out, Nick, go get me something for this headache." Robert, Nick, and Niles sat down on opposite sides of the table and filled the mayor in.

The cell members were headed to the safe house in Luella when they caught Lynn's signal to retreat. The next in command contacted agent thirty with the current development. Agent thirty, better know as Francis Johnson, replaced the phone and went into agent twenty-one's office, Barnabas Matthew. "What seems to be the problem?"

"Lynn and her lackey have been taken into custody." She took a seat in front of his desk.

"Oh, hell! I can't believe she got sloppy." Barnabas pushed away from his desk and walked toward the window. He ran his hands through his hair in a frustrated gesture. His normally perfect hair was a mess. "How did this happen?"

"According to our source, they were trying to retrieve the disk. They were sent on a wild goose chase and got caught."

"What was she doing with our missions on disk? Didn't she realize the risk? I knew we shouldn't have trusted her. I had my reservations from the beginning. Now I have to go in and clean up the mess!" He slammed his fist on the desk. "Where is the disk now?"

Frances quickly became defensive. "Listen, I thought she was on our side. We did remove that information from her file." She stood up and leaned on the desk to get in his face.

"That doesn't matter now. What did your source say?" He sat back down and took a couple deep breaths.

"My source believes one of our operatives passed the disk to Sam Gabriels. He was seen following her two days ago in Luella."

Barnabas looked stunned by the name. "Did you just say Sam Gabriels?" He swallowed noticeably and sank back into his chair.

Frances assessed her partner with curiosity. "Yes. What's going on? Why is she so special?"

"The fact is, we now know she's the Alliance leader's daughter. I'm not sure why Hilary told me to plant a tail on her four years ago," He leaned back in his chair in concentration. "Got any ideas?"

"I'm thinking. What do we know about her?" She tapped a finger to her lips in thought.

Barnabas Matthew tried to remember the intelligence he received in a diplomatic pouch. Included were photos, neighbors' names, teachers, and her class schedule. "She's twenty-one years old, a straight "A" student studying political science, outgoing, and easy to anger. She works out daily and we haven't seen any unusual activity. She has three main friends Jamie Hutchins and Nick and Niles McGovens. They meet every Saturday at the Pizza Plaza in Luella. She was hard to tail and her friends are just as smart. Her father is also the mayor of Luella and her mother is a botanist who works independently for the government."

"That's nothing out of the ordinary. What's our next step?"

"We're going to Luella to do some house hunting. Contact our best operatives and have them meet us at safe house number five by twenty-two hundred." He rose from his chair and gathered his gear from a hidden closet. "One more thing. Move up the time table on the next target."

"I'm on it. Do you want me to contact Hilary?" Frances asked with a note of fear.

"Not yet. Let's see what we run into first. I don't want to involve her just yet." Hilary was the last person he wanted to contact. She'd have him eliminated in a minute. He needed insurance and he needed it fast. Where was that girl hiding?

CHAPTER 11

BACK IN Luella, Lynn Weston had been going through an intense interrogation and was being uncooperative. "Chief, she's not giving us anything useful. What tactic do you want to use next?" Detective Michaels was at a loss for words. He put a shoulder against the wall and crossed his ankles.

In walked his assistant, breathing hard. "Chief, your computer is beeping like crazy." Patrick rushed past his assistant and Detective Michaels followed.

"Close the door, Kane, and lock it. This might be what we're waiting for." He opened his secure e-mail from Nick. *Dad — The Mayor is safe and we now know more names from the list. Dad, try matching these names with the photo's we sent you. Don't forget that imaging software. –Nick*

"I almost forgot. Before we left, I started to run that program." He opened the program and stared at the screen. "Would you look at this?" Before him were possible matches for two suspects, Francis Johnson and Barnabas Matthew.

Kane gave out a low whistle. "Do you know what this means, Chief?"

"Yes, I do. We need to find them and fast. Should we call in Military Intel or CERT?" The chief sat there with a frown on his face. He looked up at Kane's next comment.

"I bet Robert knows who we should call and I have a feeling he's in Mantis with the mayor." Kane laughed with a sheepish grin.

"Who's Robert and how do you know he's there?" The chief assessed his detective with an air of speculation. He turned back to his computer and composed a message to Nick. Kane took a moment to explain who Robert was and what his role was in this mess.

Nick — Have Robert give us a call on a secure land line. We need to discuss how to proceed from this point. I've been told that he knows whom to call and who we're really after. –Dad

Nick's computer started beeping again with an incoming message. He glanced up at Robert with questions in his eyes. He walked away from the table, unsure of how this news would change the game. He decided to tell Aron first. "Mr. Gabriels, can I talk to you in private?" Aron got up from the table and led Nick to the other bedroom, sensing his hesitation to speak in front of Robert.

"What seems to be the problem, son?" Nick turned away for a minute, not quite sure how to word his question.

"My father knows Robert is here and wants to talk to him. How does he know? We never told him about Robert."

Aron Gabriels rubbed a hand across his chin in thought. "I'm not sure," he shrugged his shoulders. "I guess we call and find out."

They left the room to face Robert. He knew something was wrong just by the disapproving look on Nick's face. Aron nudged Nick back to his seat and turned to Robert. "We have a quandary it seems. Chief McGovens wants to talk to you. We have no idea how he knew you're here."

"I have an idea. Maybe we better call. Nick, can you set me up with a secure line?" Nick looked up from the table and was surprised by Robert's grin.

"Just give me a minute." He quickly hooked up the compact computer Robert had given them to the room phone. "All set. It'll ring directly to my dad's office."

In Luella, Chief McGovens phone rang. He looked at Detective Michaels and said, "Here we go. Hello?"

"I heard you wanted to speak to me," Robert said in a cool voice.

"Where to begin? First is the mayor nearby?" Kane was listening in via another phone.

"Yes," Robert answered.

"Next question. We have Lynn Weston and Mattie Ulysis in custody. Mattie is cooperating, but Lynn won't say anything. Someone here said you'd know whom to contact. Should we contact M.I. or CERT?"

"Maybe you should call the latter. Tell them I instructed you to call and that I need this prisoner interrogated."

"Next, is everybody safe?" He looked across the desk and Kane handed him a piece of paper. The chief read it and said, "Kane wants to know if you need help."

"Everybody's safe," Robert said with a sigh as he rubbed his forehead. "Yes, send him." Robert hung up the phone and looked around the table, his eyes locked with the questioning ones of Aron's. Here's one moment he'd dreaded since meeting Aron. He'd like him from the start and hated lying to him about his true identity.

"Is there something we need to talk about, Robert? I think you left out a few things when I met you five years ago." Aron had a disappointed look on his face.

Niles glared at Robert, then bowed his head while shaking it. *How could Sam like a guy they knew so little about?* He wondered. "Nick, Niles, why don't you go to bed and get some rest?" The twins too quickly agreed and left the room. *"What has gotten into the twins? They've never listened,"* Aron thought.

Robert held up a finger, telling Aron to wait. He quietly walked over to the door and gave a quick push. "Ouch, my nose," Nick yelled. Aron stifled a laugh and so did Robert.

"Now get some rest. If I have something to tell you, I'll let you know." He pulled the door shut and walked to the kitchen for a drink, returning quickly to the table where Aron was sitting. "I apologize. There were things I couldn't tell you when we met. First, let me reintroduce myself I'm Colonel Robert Michaels under the direction of Military Intel. Second, I report directly to Chancellor Ronin, and any information I gather is for his eyes only. Lastly, I was recruited to uncover who was ordering the murders, sabotage, and generally interfere. Military intelligence suspected you from the beginning, Aron."

"What do you mean?" Aron asked, a confused look on his face.

"Military intelligence had reason to suspect you were ordering events. I was able to clear you when you recruited me to infiltrate the cell. At the time, even I thought you were in charge. Then Lynn Weston approached said she wanted my expertise on a special project, and I realized that you weren't involved. She wanted me to obtain explosives for the harvester testing." Robert could tell Aron believed him—the man was a good judge of character.

"That explanation is good enough. Apparently, she obtained them from another source," Aron remembered the explosion a couple of days before. "Now, who's coming to help?" Aron asked inquiringly.

"My cousin, Detective Kane Michaels, was also recruited by military intelligence to keep an eye on your associates. He's in a position to hear pertinent information and help me when needed." Robert wrapped his hands around the glass waiting for the anger.

"Yes, he's in a good position. On more than one occasion my family has had Kane over for dinner. He's been a regular part of our gatherings for the last couple of years. The twins have taken to him like an older brother. That sneaky devil, I had no idea." Robert relaxed. Aron was a good man.

Robert chuckled. "I can't wait for Kane to get here. I'm sure he has some interesting stories about Sam and her friends."

Aron shared a laugh with Robert. "How about some sleep. I'll go in with the twins and you take the couch. Keep a close eye on the girls for me." He knew they'd sleep it off and wouldn't be a problem.

"That'll do. Then I can keep an eye out for Kane." With a weary smile Aron gave a wave and closed the door to the bedroom.

CHAPTER 12

ANNIE GABRIELS was awoken by the creak on the stairs. She remained quiet while swiftly reaching for the weapon in the nightstand. She searched the room for exits; the only ones were the door or the window. She crouched behind the chair within range of the door. The door slowly opened and she took aim when she saw the intruder. He looked about the room, noticed the empty bed, turned toward the chair, and came face to face with a gun. He took a step back, reaching for his own weapon. Another intruder entered the room and Annie fired, first at the closest intruder, then at the other.

There were shouts and an influx of bodies in Annie's room. The weapon was quickly knocked from her hand. She was forced to defend herself in hand-to-hand combat and broke the next intruder's nose. Annie was finally subdued, but only when she was charged by a very large man, and she got in a few good punches before she went down. She lay on the floor catching her breath while her hands and feet were tied. She was unable to move, one intruder had a knee in her back.

They carried her out under the cover of darkness. She noticed the house was torn apart. Annie was grateful Sam and Aron were both out of town. The only thing Annie kept thinking was how Sam would react to her being missing. She knew this day would come. Aron said the cell was becoming restless; the explosion earlier that week was a good example.

The two who seemed to be in charge were yelling at each other. The intruders said they couldn't find the disk and it wasn't in the house. They finally stopped arguing only to reenter the house and search again. "The girl must have it with her, wherever she is," the woman said. They left a satellite phone in Sam's room.

"She'll be back," he said smugly. "We have mommy and daddy," Orders were given to one of the operatives to keep watch over the house, and contact them immediately when Sam returned. Annie was shoved into a waiting car and taken to the McGovens farm outside Luella. Fear gripped her as she realized Aron had been captured and they were looking for Sam. *Her husband! Her child!* She thought in fear.

In the small hours of the night, Robert snapped awake, sensing someone was in the room. He reached under his pillow for his weapon and pretended to sleep. The figure stopped at the end of the couch and whispered. "Tag! You're it." Robert groaned and sat up realizing exactly who was there and disengaged his weapon.

"Kane, how long have you been standing there? Nice cloak. I didn't recognize you in civilian attire. You changed your eye and hair color, too."

"I didn't want to be recognized. I've been standing here long enough. I could have shot you. You never used to sleep so soundly. What gives?" With a frown on his face he walked to the other side of the couch.

Robert shook his head. "You've met Sam and her friends. They're not easy to follow." He leaned his head against the back of the couch.

Kane chuckled and took a seat beside him. "I have and I know what you mean. One time the chief sent me to find the twins. It took me three hours to track them down, even with my resources. I have a feeling it was a test of sorts. I finally tracked them to an old farmhouse outside Luella. They were making their own alcohol. That is one bunch of bright kids."

"Currently, we have two passed out," He pointed over his shoulder to the two sleeping figures. "Coffee, Kane?"

"Sounds like a good idea. Sam and whom else?" Kane asked with mild curiosity. They moved to the kitchen and started a pot of coffee.

"Jamie," Robert replied while he rummaged through the cupboard to find what he needed.

Kane smiled, remembering who else he found at that farmhouse, and how she was dressed. "Jamie. She's the petite blond with blue eyes, right?"

Robert gave his cousin an inquiring stare and grinned. "That's the one." Kane grabbed two cups and carried them to the table. "I brought some goodies with me and a change of clothes for you." Kane pointed to the long duffle bags next to the door.

"Thanks. I could use a shower. The last couple of days have been crazy," He ran a hand across his two-day-old stubble. "She's constantly on the move."

"Sit and tell me about it and I'll fill you in on what's happening in Luella."

Robert began to tell Kane how he found the encrypted disk in Lynn Weston's office and how Aron become unreachable. He couldn't risk being caught with the disk. That's why he started following Sam and her friends. He had to find her father and pass off the disk. "Lynn started having me followed when I wouldn't acquire the explosive she wanted, and making contact with Aron became very difficult. She must have found someone else; did you see that destruction? While following Sam, I saw Mattie trying to be buddies with her. I was able to pass off the disk and never thought she would look at it, let alone involve her friends.

"Aron was taken captive and the next thing I knew, Sam was asking for my help. Nick is such a wiz with computers and Niles . . . he's something else, it's like he has photographic memory. He also can't keep his eyes off Sam.

"Jamie can't keep her eyes off Niles and she seems just as smart as the rest. With the help of the twins, we were able to get Aron out of the water tower and back here safely. And those two," he pointed to the bed, "couldn't handle the wait and started drinking the mini-bar dry." They both started laughing. Robert left to shower and came back to finish his tale.

"Now down to the cell members and what I know about each. Up until yesterday, I only knew them by number. Sam and her friends have figured out most of their names. From what I've gathered, Mattie was recruited to watch Sam. I'm still not sure why. Lynn seems to be the commander; she gave the orders and collected the data for someone else.

"There's another guy who goes by "agent twenty-one." He's the supply guy and handled all deliveries for government transports. He can get Lynn whatever she needs except explosives. Then there's "agent thirty." She seems to be the supervisor. She made sure the mission was accomplished and reported back to agent twenty-one. I haven't been able to get much information on agent fifty, I never see her, but she has to be the brains of the operation."

"I can fill in some of the blanks as to why Mattie was sticking to Sam. You're never going to believe this," Kane shook his head when Robert waved his hand in an impatient gesture. "Mattie was watching for you. Lynn told her you were the bad guy. She was also under the impression that Lynn Weston was working for the government. We also have two other possible suspects, but they haven't been confirmed yet. The chief was still trying to locate them when I left."

Kane continued to tell Robert about the link from Lynn to the missing agent's murders based on the data Nick sent. "I wasn't aware of anything until the twins contacted the chief. My orders were to stick close to the chief and his family. I was told to watch out for any unusual occurrences. The kidnapping came as a shock and the chief acted quickly. Mattie was quick to answer when questioned. That's how I knew you were here. Sam's too smart and she knew she could trust you. Must be the Michaels charm." They both smiled, then made plans to sweep the safe houses and find their next target.

A couple of hours later, Nick and Niles crawled out of bed and heard voices in the other room. They cautiously walked over to the door and heard the male laughter. Opening the door, they saw Robert sitting with Detective Kane Michaels. Niles was the first to ask, "What are you doing here?" Niles took a closer look at Robert then glanced between the two. "So this is your cousin from the photograph on your desk? I can't believe I didn't recognize you sooner."

With a teasing note his voice Robert said to Niles, "If you took your eyes off Sam for five seconds you might have figured it out sooner." Niles left to get a cup of coffee and turned around when Kane next spoke.

"Apparently, Niles has never noticed how much Jamie watches his every move." Kane scowled down into his coffee.

"How would you know? Oh wait, you like Jamie." Niles turned away with a knowing smirk and missed Kane's clenched hands.

Jamie woke up and said, "Would you just stop with all that male testosterone. I'm trying to sleep." She promptly fell back on the bed. Kane unclenched his hands at the sight of Jamie's beautiful face. He never failed to react. Just being near her sent off warning bells in his head. The first time he met her was at the station. Nick had dragged her down when his dad got hit by a perp. He was having problems breathing, and within minutes of Jamie's arrival he was back to normal.

Aron and Nick couldn't believe their ears and just shrugged it off. Nick headed off to make breakfast and pulled Niles with him. Nick said to Niles in a stern voice, "We need them on our side. Keep your feelings to yourself for now. It's time to tell them what we learned last night."

With a sigh Niles agreed and they headed back to the other room. Nick grabbed his computer to compare the names they found with the photos taken at the Hotel Dirtron the day before. As Niles reentered the room, Aron was chatting with Kane and overheard the name of Barnabas Matthew.

Nick conveyed their findings. "We found a lead night. He's confirming the information now. We saw Barnabas Matthew and Francis Johnson names as we were leaving the building. If we're right, we have two more names for you."

Aron walked over to Nick and looked at the computer screen. He laid a hand on his shoulder. "What have you found out, Nick?"

"One of the cell members is Barnabas Matthew, supply

coordinator for all government transports to Plutonus. The other is Francis Johnson, executive assistant to Matthew." On the computer screen were the government photos and all their personnel information.

"Good work, Nick." Aron glanced over his shoulder. "Robert, Kane, take a look. I think it's time we find all the missing pieces of the puzzle. This has gone on long enough. Nick, do your magic and find what we need to take them down. I'm sorry I didn't think of this sooner." Nick was overjoyed he finally had support to do what he loved most, hacking.

CHAPTER 13

MORNING ARRIVED bright and clear. The temperature was reaching it normal low of ninety-eight degrees. When Sam opened her eyes she squinted into the light and tried to remember what had happened the night before. She groaned when she noticed two figures sitting at the table watching while they checked weapons.

"I must be dreaming or I drank more than I thought. There are two of them now," Sam said to herself as she sat up and held her head in her hands. She closed her eyes and when she opened them again, her vision cleared. "Nope, there are definitely two. Jamie, are you seeing what I am?"

"Yes, now be quiet my head is pounding." Kane and Robert were grinning from ear to ear at the spectacle before them. Even hungover they were beautiful.

Aron walked over and placed a strong cup of coffee in her hands. "Sam, drink up. We have things to do," Aron glanced over to Jamie where Niles was trying to give her a cup of coffee. She kept pushing it away. "Are you two going to be able to travel?"

"Niles, get that vile stuff away from me and hand me my bag." Niles reached over and handed Jamie her bag. She pulled out a little blue cloth bag and with Niles' help, went into the kitchen. Moments later she returned with two fresh cups and handed one to Sam. "Bottoms up. This will sober you up."

Sam smiled up at Jamie. "Cheers," she drank it all down without stopping. "Now, it's time for a hot shower." All the males moaned at the image she created in their minds.

"Jamie, what else do you have in that bag? Anything we can use?" Niles looked at Jamie questioningly.

"But of course. It's grandma's little bag of tricks," she stated and shrugged her shoulders in response to their stares.

"Let me see that. I know your grandmother." Aron took her bag and carefully laid out several different colored pouches and jars of balm. "Yes, there are things in here we can use. Jamie, I didn't realize you were that far in your studies." Aron looked at Jamie like a proud father would.

Jamie blushed and pointed at Kane. "I'll have my doctorate at the end of the term. Now who is that?"

Kane chuckled at her question. "Jamie, I'm hurt. I thought you'd remember me."

Jamie moved closer to Kane and leaned down. "Aren't your eyes normally blue?" Recognition flared in Jamie's face. "Detective Kane Michaels?"

Kane pulled out a silver wand and waved it across his eyes. "Better, Jamie?"

Jamie blushed and backed away "Much," she said.

Sam, now sober, snapped her head up and stared at the two men at the table. "Are you two brothers?" she asked, taking in the similarities same facial features and muscle build.

The two men shared a knowing look and Kane replied, "No, he's my cousin."

In the early morning daylight, Christopher Jackknife landed

from Plutonus. He was on his way to Luella to interrogate Lynn Weston. She was recently brought in as a suspect in numerous murders and suspected sabotage of government transports. He'd received the call late last the night before. Under orders from the general, he was to leave with all haste and report back immediately. He was also informed that if Colonel Michaels needed additional assistance, he was to give it, no questions asked.

C.J. hoped Ms. Weston would cooperate and make this job easier, but from what Chief McGovens told him she had been very uncooperative. C.J. knew that would all change once he'd entered the room. He was glad they called him back to Pretoria; Plutonus was starting to depress him. He preferred the clean smelling air, the flowers, and the clear skies. He took a deep breath and enjoyed the fresh morning air, and with lightness to his step he continued on his way.

He remembered that on his last visit to Luella M.I. had him interrogate a witness to the provincial governor's murder. The poor man had his mind wiped clean. The only memories he could find were from his childhood. Whoever did that job really messed him up.

C.J. walked up to the desk at the Luella Police department and flashed his credentials. A gentleman in his fifties greeted him with a hardy handshake and happiness in his gray eyes. C.J. assumed this was the police chief.

"Christopher Jackknife, I presume? Chief Patrick McGovens at your service."

"Call me C.J.," he said, returning the handshake and thinking he really liked the guy's friendly manner. He rarely meets cooperative individuals.

"Well C.J., we'll go to my office and I'll fill you in on the suspect." C.J. felt the chief had a lot to tell him, and he wouldn't pry unless it was necessary. He shortened his stride to keep pace with Chief McGovens. He was tall at six foot and had to remind himself that others weren't.

"I understand she's being difficult. M.I. has filled me in on what they know to date." They reached the privacy of the chief's office before he said any more.

"Then you probably know more than I do." Chief McGovens explained to him what they knew and then escorted him to interrogation where Lynn Weston was waiting. He never mentioned his sons' involvement.

He took a seat across from Ms. Weston. "We can do this the easy way or the hard way, Ms. Weston. Which do you prefer?"

Lynn was quick to reply with menace in her voice. "I refuse to tell you anything." She wouldn't look at him and kept her gaze down cast.

With a smirk C.J. went to work. He grabbed her face and stared directly into her eyes. With a start he jumped back from the table. "Damn, why wasn't that in her file?" He pointed at Lynn in anger, his eyes boring into hers. "I'll deal with you in a minute." It seems protected government files were being tampered with. He stalked out of the interrogation room to call his commander. He'd never had to break through a mind wiper. It could be dangerous to him as well as her.

Robert moved away from the table. "Kane, gather up the gear and we'll check out the safe houses in the area. There was someone staying there last night watching the alley. The rest of you can head back to the Luella Police Department. Kane and I will be along shortly. I have a feeling Mr. Matthew and Ms. Johnson aren't in town."

Aron watched Kane and Robert gear up. "Are you sure we shouldn't stick together?"

He glanced up and told Aron in no uncertain terms, "No, it would be best if you head back. Kane and I can handle this part on our own."

Aron rubbed a hand across his face and sighed understanding his meaning. The glint in their eyes had him stepping back. "I guess your right. It'll be safer to travel this morning. Come on kids, it's time to leave."

Sam was the first to say something. "What if they need our skills?" She pointed to Robert and Kane. "We've been training for years for just this type of event."

"We're just going to the safe houses to determine where exactly Mr. Matthew and Ms. Johnson are and clean house." He gave a knowing look to Kane, ignoring the hard stare from Sam.

"Sam, they can handle this, now move. Gather your things, we have a pod to catch." Aron gave her his sternest look and she started packing her bag forcefully.

After seeing the others off, Robert and Kane moved toward the alley of the first safe house. "What was all that talk about training?"

"I've only heard about some of the basics from the chief. They're pretty quiet concerning their training," Kane shrugged and kept moving. "I've seen the twins challenge a few of the better officers. They have a very interesting technique. There have been many days when the range was closed for hours and out would walk the four of them. They'd be completely outfitted in full tactical gear and loaded with weapons I'd never seen."

"Weapons training, martial arts, and diversionary tactics. What do you think Aron's training them for?" Robert inquired.

"Who knows, but I do know they're good." They reached the first building and Robert scanned it to get a feel for the layout. The building was straightforward; apartments ran from the front to the back of the building, separated by a main staircase. A fire escape ran along the back of the building. The only apartment currently in use was on the top floor.

"I'll go in first. They know me. You follow right behind." They entered the back hallway and headed up the stairs, keeping close to the shadows. Robert began to scan the room from outside to get a better feel for the room. There were only two cell members, not the ones they were looking for. *This will be easy,* Robert thought. He motioned the number to Kane, and he acknowledged.

With weapon drawn, he signaled to Kane to stand on the other side of the door. Kane attached a small device to the door lock and pushed the remote timer. "Special delivery," he said.

There was an explosion and the door opened. The cell members were stunned momentarily when Robert tried to enter the room. Shots started flying. A bullet nicked his left arm, causing a stinging sensation. He retreated back into the hall where he saw one of the cell move behind the door. Robert signaled to Kane to hold fire. He aimed his weapon at the wall and fired. "One down, one to go!" He figured it was payback for the nick on his arm.

While the other cell member was distracted, Kane entered the room and fired. The cell member slumped to the floor with a thud. "Just like old times. Right, Robert?" He gave a nod in agreement. Kane noticed the packed bags by the door. "These bags make it look like they were about to leave."

Robert checked through the other rooms, then moved to search the desk. He saw a notepad near the phone. "They were headed to Luella. Seems they have another mission. What could they possible want in Luella?"

Kane had made arrangement with the local police department to clean up the mess, and they skirted past them. The two men headed to the next safe house. As they expected, it was empty and the same message had been scrawled on the notepad. This had to be big if they were clearing the safe houses and gathering in Luella.

Did they know about the disk? Did they know Aron was gone? Could he keep Sam safe? These and other thoughts ran through Robert's mind on the ride back to Luella.

CHAPTER 14

TWO HOURS later, the mayor, Sam, Jamie, Nick, and Niles were escorted from the pod station to the Luella Police Department by military officers. Chief McGovens was waiting with C.J. in a conference room discussing Lynn Weston's unlisted gift.

"There they are now," The chief walked over to hug his troublesome sons. "Let me take a look at you. Good, no new bumps or bruises. Your grandmother was so worried that she's been baking up a storm. I had to bring some into work." He patted his slightly rounded stomach and pointed to the pile of cookies on the table. "Help yourselves. There's also fresh coffee. Sam, Jamie, you're looking a little worse for the wear."

From the tone in his voice, Sam and Jamie knew they were busted. He could always tell when they'd been drinking must be a cop thing. Sam was quick to quip and gave him a peck on the cheek. "We haven't had much sleep in the last twenty-four hours." They took a seat at the table and each grabbed a cookie, facing away from his knowing gaze.

"There's more to that story, Patrick. I'll fill you in later. What have you learned from Ms. Weston?" Aron took a seat next to the stranger. Chief McGovens made a quick introduction to the group. "This is C.J. from M.I. He was sent to interrogate Ms. Weston and we ran into a problem."

Aron assessed the man sitting next to him. He was a typical military man, with short black hair, a tall muscular build, a deep voice, and eyes as shrewd as a cat's. "It's just a temporary set back. I'll get through her block yet," C.J. said with a scowl.

Aron looked confused. "I thought you could read anything or anyone?"

"That's correct, but Ms. Weston's file never mentioned she has the psychic ability to block and wipe minds. The information was conveniently erased," he replied briskly.

"But how is that possible? I thought all records were secured on Plutonus." Aron and Patrick noticed C.J. staring intensely at Nick and Niles. Nick looked down at the table, ignoring the conversation flowing around him.

"Obviously a few extremely exceptional hacks are able to break past the firewall. Nick, look at me and tell them." C.J. stated his request in a harsh tone to Nick.

"Would you stop looking through my mind? It's a little creepy." Nick looked directly into his pale yellow eyes.

"Son, how long have you known about this back door?" Chief McGovens asked, standing behind the chair as he placed his hands on Nick's shoulders.

Nick was still staring at C.J. and answered truthfully. "About a year ago, I designed a code breaker program. I created it just to see if I could. I never meant to cause a problem," He shrugged his shoulders. "Guess it worked better than I thought. I didn't tell anyone for fear they would take the program and remove me from Pretoria."

"I suppose you can get into any government computer with this program." His father started to sound angry.

"The computers here on Pretoria and on Plutonus are

accessible," Nick said as he bowed his head. "Enough! I can't handle anymore. You're giving me a headache."

C.J. was still looking at Nick, but then he closed his eyes. "You have a very bright son there, Chief McGovens. I haven't met many minds like his."

Jamie rushed over to Nick's side. "Niles, go get me some hot tea and be quick about it."

"Next time, give me some warning before you do that again C.J." There was more anger and concern in Patrick's voice.

"Sorry, just had to make sure he was telling the truth." He sat there with his eyes still closed and rubbed a hand across his forehead. He searched his leather jacket for the bottle of pills he always carried.

Niles reentered the room and Jamie was rifling through her bag. She pulled out a small red cloth bag and carefully added the mixture to the tea. "Here, Nick. Drink this. It'll offset what he did to you." She shot a look in C.J.'s direction. He could feel her anger.

"Thanks, Jamie. I knew I could count on you." With a grateful smile Nick downed the mixture and ate another cookie. "Grandma always did make the best cookies." He said through a mouthful.

C.J. finally opened his eyes and saw the red bag on the table. "What did you give him? He recovered so quickly."

"It's just a mixture of natural herbs that chemically react with the tea. This bags' intent was for the common stress headache," Jamie proudly answered, but was none to happy about the current condition of her friend.

"Do you think I could get a cup of that?" C.J. asked curiously. He was up to trying anything to get rid of imprint headaches. The pills the doctors gave him weren't working anymore. He wasn't sure anything would at this point in his life.

She watched him for a moment and could sense his pain. When they first entered the room he was tossing back pills. She felt sorry for him and figured who would it hurt. "Niles, could you please go get me another cup?" When Niles returned, Jamie made another batch for C.J.

He drank it gratefully, then faced Aron. "Mayor, I've also been asked to do a psychic evaluation on you, but only if you don't cooperate."

"I'll cooperate and tell you everything you want to know. I have nothing to hide," Mayor Gabriels calmly told C.J. everything he knew of the alliance and splinter cell. By the time Aron Gabriels was done with his accounting, Robert and Kane Michaels returned with the news that Mr. Matthew and Ms. Johnson were somewhere in Luella.

"C.J., it's nice to see you again. It's been awhile," Robert shook hands with him in greeting.

"Yes, it has. After that last debriefing I didn't expect to see you or your cousin again. Now what did you find out? Your superiors are getting nervous."

"We have a meeting time, but not the place. Kane and I did a quick sweep of the safe houses and they were all empty. C.J., have you been able to crack Ms. Weston?"

"No, but I'm going to try again. Kane, would you like to sit in? Maybe act as a distraction?"

"Absolutely, if you think it will help," Kane replied.

Jamie watched and listened. She nudged Sam and reached into her bag. They slipped out of the room to the vending machines.

Sam waited until the room was clear before she asked, "What do you need Jamie? I know you have an idea."

"Remember that little white bag I told you about?" Jamie turned to get another cup of tea. She pulled the bag out from under her shirt, dropped the powder in the cup, and stirred.

"Yes, but you said you'd never use it," They giggled at the thought of Lynn Weston babbling all of her secrets. "Now, how do we get it to her?"

With a knowing smile Jamie said, "Leave it to me. Now, hurry back. We have to intercept Kane before he goes in there. C.J. will know we're up to no good if we see him first." She pointed to the interrogation room where Ms. Weston had been kept waiting.

"Perfect timing," Sam whispered as Kane approached them.

"Where have you two been?" Kane asked, eyeing the two conspirators suspiciously.

"We thought Lynn might like some fresh tea to drink. Could you take it to her?" Jamie batted her long lashes at him and flipped her hair behind her ear. Sam could only think *Go Jamie!* She finally understood her full allure.

"Sure, why not." He took the cup with speculation and entered the interrogation room.

"Wish I could be a fly on that wall. This is going to be good," Sam said with a grin on her face. "The things we do for our government."

As they reentered the conference room, Sam noted the wound on Robert's arm. She rushed to his side. "When did this happen?"

He pushed her hand away as if it burned. "It's just a scratch."

She started tugging at his jacket to get a better look, but he wouldn't budge. "Take off your jacket. Jamie!" Sam called over her shoulder.

"Right here. Niles we need hot water and clean bandages." Sam started to remove Robert's jacket, but he pulled away again. "What do you think you're doing?" He flinched at the pain.

"We're fixing that arm," She glared at him her lips forming a thin line.

"Robert, let the girls tend to you. They know what they're doing," Aron stated calmly. Robert relented and winced when Sam used a little more force than necessary to remove his jacket. The twins laughed at the spectacle and gazed away when he glared at them.

CHAPTER 15

LYNN WESTON looked up when Detective Michaels and C.J. entered the room. "Here. I thought you might like something to drink." Kane placed the cup in front of her.

"At least someone around here has manners." She took a tentative drink, then another.

"Are you ready to cooperate now?" Kane asked. C.J. walked around the edge of the room watching her drink the tea.

She finally put the cup down and leaned back in the chair in a relaxed pose. "I told you already. I won't tell you anything." She started to giggle and put a hand to her mouth. C.J. sensed the change in her brain waves and moved over to the table curious about the change. The doors she had closed in her mind were opening and he was able to easily read her.

Her next words left both men stunned. "Did I ever tell you why I became involved with the cell?"

When the shock wore off, C.J. started asking questions and Kane slipped out of the room to find Jamie. He found her in the conference room and quickly pulled her out of her chair into a bear hug. Jamie stood frozen for a minute then melted into his arms, closing her eyes, and enjoying the feeling of his arms.

"You did it, Jamie." He pulled away, but kept his hands on her waist. "Whatever you put in that tea worked! She's telling C.J.

everything." He gave Jamie another hug and a quick kiss with a twinkle in his blue eyes. "I have to get back, but when this is over I'm taking you out to celebrate."

Jamie just nodded, collapsed into the nearest chair, and started fanning her face. "Wow! If I only knew it was that easy to get his attention."

Robert said with a brisk voice, "What just happened here?" He was in conversation with Aron and missed part of what went on. His cousin was in and out in a flash and Jamie looked about to faint.

"Jamie just saved the day with a little never fail truth serum." Sam was standing near Jamie with a smug know-it-all-look. Aron let out a roaring laugh and slapped the table.

Lynn continued to tell them how she joined the cell to help change the way the government handled things on both planets. She was approached by Mr. Matthew and Ms. Johnson because they found out about her talent of wiping and blocking memories. That was five years ago and she'd been the field commander from the beginning. She was instructed to pick up a diplomatic pouch every two weeks that could only be opened with her thumbprint. The pouch contained information on the target and enough funds to accomplish the task. There was also a list of cell members suited for the task.

"Who decided on the targets?" C.J. asked, making notes on a small computer.

"I don't honestly know," Lynn said with a frown.

"Whom did you report to?"

"I reported back to Mr. Matthew and Ms. Johnson," she said nonchalantly.

"Would that be Barnabas Matthew and Francis Johnson?" He asked, only for clarification purposes.

"Yes, they supplied me with whatever supplies I needed. I used others for the actual missions," Lynn looked directly into C.J.'s eyes. "Do you know you have nice eyes? What a unique color."

C.J. continued with his questions ignoring her comment. "Did you have a list of other cell operatives and targets?"

"Yes, they were on disk in my office, but it came up missing. I believe Robert took it and gave it to that Gabriels girl." Lynn was looking a little weary and started rubbing her temples.

"You look a little tired. Why don't I have an officer take you to a room for a rest?" C.J. showed some concern, thinking they may need her for more information later.

"That sounds really good. Do you think I might get a bite to eat and some more of that delicious tea?" she asked Kane.

"I'll see what I can do."

An officer entered and escorted her to a secure cell. C.J. put his head in his hands and breathed out a huge sigh of relief. The chief followed not long after she left. "Is everything okay, C.J.?"

"I'm a little confused. Why did she start being so cooperative?" C.J. had a stressed expression on his face.

The chief moved toward the door. "If you'll come with me, I have someone to reintroduce you to. She saved my life one day."

Kane moved from his position leaning against the interrogation room wall. "She's got some pretty special talents."

"Wait, she's the one with the red pouch," *and gorgeous body* he thought. She had hair of gold, eyes of blue, and he sensed her healing touch.

"Yes, she had me bring in the tea for Ms. Weston. At first I didn't think anything about it, she and Sam intercepted me in the hall. She finished the tea so quick, and then it dawned on me that Jamie used one of her little tricks."

They entered the room and C.J. saw Jamie sitting in deep discussion with Sam. "That was some little trick. Does the government know about it?"

"I doubt it," the chief stated. "Her grandmother invented it along time ago in order to find out if her children were telling the truth. It seems Jamie has tweaked it a little. She's made it taste better and you don't realize it's in your drink."

The three of them watched Jamie and Sam. "I thought Aron was joking when he said Jamie had things we could use." Kane shook his head, remembering two hungover young ladies that morning. They looked just fine now.

"I have a new respect for what the alliance is trying to accomplish. The government would've taken her idea, maybe even her, and I'd be out of a job." C.J. smiled at the thought wondering what other hidden talents were in this room.

Robert and Aron looked up when the others entered the room. C.J. turned his attention from Sam and Jamie and focused on Robert. "Robert, Ms. Weston is under the impression that you took a disk from her office. Do you currently have it in your possession?"

Robert looked in Sam's direction. "No, I gave it to Sam to give to her father, Aron."

C.J. posed the question in Sam's direction. "Where is the disk now?"

Quickly understanding how C.J. worked, Sam gave him a direct look when she answered. "The disk is well hidden. Nick has a partially decoded disk here and the original is at my home."

"I'll take Sam to pick it up," Robert was quick to volunteer. "The fewer officers involved, the better. I can protect her with the other cell members in Luella. Aron should stay put and out of sight. They may not realize he's missing yet."

Chief McGovens put his thought into words. "I like the idea, but I would prefer to place some plain clothes on the street near the Gabriels' home."

Kane nodded his head. "I agree. You shouldn't go in alone. Remember, the city has eyes."

Robert relented. "Fine, but only two officers. No more," They left by underground tunnels that led to a door near the pod station. "Stay close and alert." He took Sam's hand in his and pulled her close to his side. Sam glanced down at their intertwined fingers. She felt a measure of awareness run along the side of her body as it brushed against his.

Annie Gabriels passed out on the way to the McGovens farm, only to awaken in the dark. She took in her location and realized she wasn't on the farm anymore, but was on a transport ship. She heard whispered conversations from the same two who were arguing earlier. She strained to hear and only picked up a few words—enough to know they were talking about her daughter and someone named Hilary.

"We searched that house from top to bottom and didn't find a thing. Where could she have hidden that disk? This makes me so mad it could spit fire." Johnson was having a hard time sitting still and kept getting up.

"We have to be patient. She'll turn up sooner or later. If my hunch is right that operative is with her, and he'll lead her right to us. Hilary is going to pitch a big fit when she finds out what's going on." Matthew smiled and thought *it's not his head that is going to be on the chopping block.*

"How can you be so calm? I can't stand to be confined for so long. Can't we land and just go find her?" Frances Johnson started to bite her nails in frustration.

"It shouldn't be long now," He confidently reached for the satellite phone and it rang in his hand. "What's the status?"

"They just exited the pod station and are headed toward the house. I'm moving out. She's accompanied by that operative and two officers in plain clothes."

"No, keep her in sight. I want to know her every move," he said with an edge to his voice. "I'll give her enough time to find our phone and the disk, and then I'll call."

CHAPTER 16

THEY REACHED the Gabriels residence in no time. As they approached the house, Sam realized something was wrong she stopped on the walkway. "The porch light is on."

Robert tugged on her arm and continued forward, trying to get out of the open. "What's so unusual about that?"

Sam tugged right back and stopped again stomping her foot down. "Mom never turns it on until late and turns it off first thing in the morning."

Robert sensed her reluctance to proceed sighed, "I'll take a look around. The house is empty. We'll go in. It's not safe out here."

He slipped his arm around her shoulder and moved her toward the now empty house. Sam opened the door and called out, "Mom, I'm back." There was no answer. She took a step back and bumped into Robert. The house had been trashed. There was computer paper everywhere, disks were scattered, and pictures had been removed for the walls. The furniture had been ripped apart and the computer was smashed to pieces. She wandered through the house in a daze and continued yelling for her mom. She hurried up the stairs to her parents' room first, the chair had been overturned and there was blood staining the carpet in several places. Robert quickly pulled her out and down the hall to check the other rooms. She entered her own room last. There was a message on the mirror.

Sam — If you want to see your parents alive, get the disk. Wait for my call and don't leave the house, I'm watching you.

There was a phone taped beside it. Her knees buckled and her hands went to her face. He grabbed her before she fell. Robert turned her into his arms and held her as her body tightened in anger. He moved them toward the bed and gathered her closer until she calmed down. He breathed in her strawberry scented hair and placed a kiss there, then her forehead in reassurance. What did he know about comforting women? He had little time for female companionship in the service, let alone anything longer than a one-night stand. *What do I do?* He wondered.

"Sam, it's going to be okay. We'll find your mom and bring her home safe." Sam gazed up into his face. That did it. He couldn't resist the sorrow he saw in her eyes, and moved his gaze lower to her lips. He leaned down and gave her a gentle kiss, just brushing his own lips against hers. Before he realized what was happening, Sam had pulled him down for a bone-melting kiss. She was kissing him!

His senses, which were barely alert, reminded him of where they were and he pulled back reluctantly from the kiss. He saw the passion and fear in her emerald eyes and moved to stand up, placing Sam on the bed creating distance between them. He tried to gather his thoughts. "We need to let the others know. Where's the disk, sweetheart? I know you put it somewhere they couldn't find it."

She took a moment to calm her breathing then climbed off the bed and righted her desk chair. She smiled back liking the term of endearment. "I put it where they wouldn't think to look." She pulled the vent grate off and reached inside. He was right behind her and put his hands on her waist to hold her steady. She turned around in his arms with the disk in hand. Looking down into his eyes she said, "Thanks for everything."

"No problem. You do know we can't go back to the station?" Sam nodded her understanding. "We better go make that call." Robert grabbed the phone and disk as she led the way to the kitchen.

Robert made his call to C.J. while Sam searched through the fridge. When Robert hung up she was preparing sandwiches. "Would you like one?" She held up a plate with a huge sandwich and chips on it.

"I could use a bite to eat. About what happened up stairs, I shouldn't have done that. I need to keep my head clear." He felt guilty. She was innocent and he could tell from her hesitant touch.

Sam was staring down at the counter. "Don't worry about it. I was upset and you were there."

Ouch that hurt, he thought, but he deserved it. He couldn't believe how mature she was being. He'd seen soldiers crack under less pressure. "They're already on the way. They should be by in about twenty minutes with my computer. I'm going to have him decode the disk completely and make a copy to take back to C.J. and his dad." A short time later there was a knock at the door. Sam jumped and Robert swiftly moved toward the front door with weapon drawn and looked out the window.

"Sam, it's me, Nick. Open the door," With a signal from Robert, she opened the door. Taking in the sight of the house, Nick turned to her. "Are you alright?" He moved into the room as she closed the door.

"I'm okay. This happened before we arrived." Nick dropped his bag and gave Sam a hug. She hugged him tight in helpless frustration.

"Hey, I'm here now and I brought everything we need. Where's the original disk?" He rubbed a hand down her back trying to comfort her.

Sam was pulled away quickly by Robert's strong grip and pushed behind him. "It's right here." He was holding the disk up in one hand and had his weapon in the other. Sam and Nick were astonished at his behavior. Nick put his hands in the air and took a step back.

"Robert, put that gun down it's just me. Look, your computer is in my bag." He pointed to the bag on the floor. Robert never took his eyes off him, making Nick nervous.

"Slide the bag over to Sam. Remove the computer and boot the system. Open the program called Ladder and enter the code "gamma" when it prompts you. If it doesn't take it, you're a dead man." Nick had only met a few soldiers in his young life, but he'd seen that look before. It meant stay put or else and he wasn't moving.

Robert's computer made a beeping noise and Sam hurriedly entered the code. "Robert, put the gun down. It took the code, here, look." She put the computer in front of him and he lowered the gun. She moved to Nick's side in a show of unity.

"Okay, now get to work. I don't know how much time we have," Robert handed both computers and the disk to Nick. "While Nick is decoding and transferring the data, I'm going to do a sweep of the house." Sam watched Robert leave the room then turned to Nick.

Nick was the first to speak. "What was that about?"

Biting her nails she answered, "I'm really not for sure. Maybe he's just being cautious."

Nick reached back into his bag. "I brought you some of grandma's cookies. She came into the station to check on us. Lord, it took some convincing to get her to let me leave. Dad almost had to restrain her." She started to laugh at the picture he painted. He could always make her laugh she really needed that right now.

"I just imagine the tongue lashing your father's getting. Did anyone else come with you?" Sam asked, a hopeful note in her voice.

Nick intently worked on the disk and watched the monitor as he answered, "Kane's around here somewhere. When we exited the pod he disappeared."

Sam paced the kitchen, then decided to clean up some of the mess. Nick made quick work decoding and copying the disk. Robert walked back in the kitchen with an armload of devices. He proceeded to the sink and turned on the water, while Nick and Sam were watching him. "The house is all clear. Are you done, Nick?"

Nick quickly replied, "Just finishing." He handed Robert the original and stored the other in his bag along with the two computers.

"Take that disk back to the police station. C.J. knows what to do with it. I heard you say Kane was around?"

"Yes, he's somewhere outside," said as he shrugged his shoulders.

"Good. He'll make sure you return safely." He still had his cool mask on, the one he'd seen earlier that meant all business and made Nick shiver.

He gave Sam one last hug and whispered in her ear. "Be safe, Sam. Grandma said to remember your strengths."

"Nick, take care. Tell everyone to hang in there, we're stronger together." Sam watched out the window and saw Kane join up with him halfway down the street.

They were sitting at the table when the phone rang. Sam reached for the phone, took a deep breath, and then answered. "Hello?"

A mans voice responded. "I see you found our message. Now listen well. Take the disk to the McGovens farm outside Luella. You know the place. Be there by four o'clock. Wait there for further instructions." The phone clicked off and Sam moved away from the table. She turned around Robert was there he took her shoulders in his hands.

"Sam, tell me what he said," he demanded gently shaking her.

She swallowed hard and wrapped her hands around her waist. "We are to go to the McGovens farm. How long have they been watching me?" She looked into his eyes for answers. "I haven't been there in over a year . . . since just after I met Mattie."

He saw the confusion in her face. "I'll figure that out later. I need to contact C.J. and Kane. We need to leave," He glanced at his watch and saw it was already three-thirty. He took Sam's hand and led her to the door. "I'll call on the way and have Kane meet us there."

The two officers followed close behind and on to the pod. Robert called Kane from the there. "Meet us at the McGovens farm. Something is not right. Did you and Nick make it back with the disk?"

"We had an escort waiting for us. Nick handed it to C.J. himself. The trip back was uneventful. If I'm not there in time be careful, cousin."

"There's no need to worry about me. I'll see you shortly." He hung up and took a seat next to Sam. He placed his arm around her and forced her head on his shoulder. "Try and rest."

CHAPTER 17

ARON LISTENED intently to Kane's conversation and sensed the tension in his voice. What could Robert be telling him? As soon as he hung up Aron was first to speak. "What's happening?"

He turned to look at the group knowing his news would shock them. "Robert and Sam are to go to the McGovens farm. He has a feeling something is wrong, I'm to meet him there." By the astonished looks on Sam's friends' faces he was right and knew it will not be easy leaving them behind.

Aron quickly rose to his feet. "I'm going with you. That's my daughter they've been watching. How did I not know?" He ran a hand across his face in frustration. They'd spent years keeping her out of the public eye. He taught her everything he knew and more.

"I would prefer it if you stayed here." Aron gave him a look that could kill. "Okay, only you. No others and I mean that. If Robert is right this could go bad real quick and I can't be watching out for you three."

Niles was on his feet now. "Come on Kane, you know we work as a team. We know every square foot of that farm and had endless training there. You can't leave us out." Aron had arranged training sights around Luella; he said it would sharpen their skills. The farm was one location they knew especially well grandpa

McGovens made sure their hiding spots were never discovered. Their father assisted Aron on one maneuver he had enlisted several officers for a training mission. The four of them were dressed in full gear and had finished well before the others. The chief was in the process of revising the academies program.

"No, you're not going. The three of you will be safer here. I don't have time to argue. Aron, it's time to go." He walked purposefully toward the door not looking back. He knew he wouldn't be able to leave them behind if he did. And what was with the training again?

"It will take a good twenty minutes to get there even by car. I hope they make it. I'm with Kane this time. You three will be staying here where I can keep a close eye on you. This is not your time." Chief McGovens followed Kane and Aron out the door leaving three disgruntled friends stuck in the conference room. He motioned to two of his officers to stand guard.

Nick watched them walk out and waited for the door to close. He pulled out Robert's computer and another bag of cookies. Niles went to the door opened it a crack, then closed and locked it.

"I can't believe this, we could have helped!" Jamie started to rant.

"I wish there was a way out of here, but I've seen the building plans. Dad actually put guards at the door." Niles walked over behind his brother to see what he was doing.

"No need to worry. I still have Robert's computer, we'll just listen in and track their position." Nick grinned up at his brother.

Jamie rushed over to join them. "His computer does that?"

"Didn't you notice the tracer he put on Sam the other day?" Nick asked Niles, who noticed everything about Sam.

"She was rubbing her arm when she came out of the boutique,"

Realization dawned on his face. "That's how he knew we were in Mantis."

"She did have a red mark on her arm the next day. I can't believe it. I wonder what the range is on the device." Jamie was even more curious now. She would be able to keep an eye on Sam.

Nick booted the Ladder program and entered Robert's password. "We'll find out soon enough."

Robert and Sam reached the farmhouse with the two officers. They positioned themselves around the farm easily out of sight. They went in the house with an old key that was taped under the porch step. Robert checked his watch. "It's almost four o'clock," he said as he walked to the window. "I wonder what's keeping Kane?"

Sam moved over to the couch and took a seat then got up to start pacing. "Maybe he just got held up." *By my friends,* she thought and almost laughed. This was one mission they shouldn't be separated on in grandpa McGovens stories they always worked together.

He grabbed her by the waist and hauled her up against him. They were a perfect fit. "Sam, sweetheart, quit pacing," Sam couldn't stop the warmth that was spreading from her head to her toes she leaned into him accepting more. Something about his touch had done that since she met him. Never before had she had these sensations. The warmth of his breath on her ear turned her knees weak. "Why did your dad call you Samantha at the hotel?"

"He knows I hate to be called that. It's his way of throwing me off guard. He knows I'll respond." He rocked her slowly and feathered light kisses along her neck. He liked her response to him, too. She moved her head to the side giving him better access and put her hand up to caress his cheek. Robert's phone rang breaking the spell. With a grunt Robert moved away and reached for his phone. "Michaels," he answered curtly.

"Did I catch you at a bad time, cousin?" Kane gave a laugh.

"You could say that. What's taking you so long? Time's almost up."

"We should be there shortly. Ran into a small detour and had to do some fast talking." He couldn't forget the look on their faces, he understood about their dynamics. He'd do anything to protect his sister and his cousin.

"Well hurry up. Something isn't right." Sam was sitting in the window seat staring out at the vast fields lost in thought. She looked up when she heard and saw the transport ship.

"Robert, we have company." She kept an eye on the ship that began to hover between the two barns.

"Kane, I need you now. We have an unauthorized transport about to land."

He moved toward the window as the kidnapper's phone rang. "Damn, I hate when this happens. I wish these cars went faster."

"If we lose connection, get to my computer and run the Ladder program. Nick knows the password. I planted a tracer on Sam awhile ago, when I kept losing her," he told Kane.

"I got it. Good luck, Robert."

She hung up the other phone with fear in her eyes. "They want us to go outside and get on the transport. They won't tell me where my mom is, what are we going to do?"

"We're going to do exactly what they want, follow it through. At this point they don't know C.J. has a copy of the disk." He grabbed her hand, brought it to his lips for a kiss keeping his eyes locked on hers. "Trust me." Robert saw the fire start to burn in her emerald eyes and knew it was time to go.

They walked out the door, her hand in his, toward the waiting transport. Robert did a scan of the farm and saw an operative hiding in the field, he moved up behind them. "Don't panic, but we have company. Keep your eyes on the transport and what ever you do don't stop walking." She gave a nod in understanding. The operative moved up behind him and removed his numerous weapons. He shrugged when Sam's eyes widened at the pile.

When the transport door opened they entered and saw her mom with a gun pointed at her head. Robert took a hold of Sam's arm to restrain her from going to her mom. To their left a gruff voice said, "Show me the disk or she dies," Robert produced the disk for inspection. "Now take a seat over there,"

With unshed tears in her eyes Sam moved to take a seat never taking her eyes off her mother, Robert moved in next to her. "Get rid of her." The one in charge said and pointed at Annie Gabriels. "We have what we need."

Annie was roughly pushed off the transport. Through the window Sam saw the two officers assist her mother and her father's car entered the drive. She turned to face Robert and saw him looking out the window. He leaned down to whisper reassuring words in her ear.

"Here, load this disk and verify the information." The man with the gruff voice commanded as the transport lifted off.

The woman did as he directed. "This is it. I can't believe the information she put on here." She tapped a few keys, opening file after file. He signaled to the pilot to take them out of orbit and meet the ship to Plutonus.

Sam wasn't sure what to make of this turn of events and feared she would never see Pretoria again. Robert put his arm around her and told her, "Rest it will be awhile before we reach our destination. I have a plan but the timing has to be perfect."

In a low whisper she asked, "Will I ever see home again?"

"Look at me, sweetheart," She looked up into his sparkling blue eyes. "I guarantee it."

In another part of Luella three friends listened to the confrontation. Niles rushed to the door of the conference room and yanked it open. "Where's my father?" The two officers were startled by Niles.

"He is in his office with that interrogator." One of the officers answered attempting to stop him with a restraining hand. Niles eyes flashed steel he quickly moved grabbing the officers wrist. He twisted and maneuvered around him leaving the officer screaming in agony.

He ran down the hall and didn't bother to knock. "Son, what's the meaning of this intrusion?" The chief stood up abruptly hearing the commotion in the hall.

"They've taken her off Pretoria. Kane and Aron didn't make it in time. How can we keep her safe now? I knew we should have gone with them." Patrick saw the anguish in his eyes and didn't know what to say.

"Hold on," C.J. put up a hand. "How do you know this?"

Niles stared at C.J. with eyes glistening. "We have Robert's computer. He put a tracer on her a couple of days ago. Nick discovered his program called the Ladder. We were able to hear their conversation and know their current location. We have to help them, please." She means everything to us he thought.

Jamie and Nick had joined behind Niles with the same expressions. The Chief's phone rang he answered with a note of dread in his voice "Hello? I understand Kane," He placed his hand over the receiver. "C.J., Kane would like to talk with you."

He took the phone and listened to Kane. "I can be there shortly, my pilot is on standby. I'll bring the computer with me. It seems Nick was already tracking them."

"Do you have the warrants ready for Barnabas Matthew and Francis Johnson?" Kane asked.

"I do. The chief and I just finished them. I'll see you shortly." He handed the phone back to Chief McGovens. "Detective Michaels has just confirmed what Niles said. They reached the farm just as the transport was leaving, Mrs. Gabriels is safe and an officer is escorting them to the medical center."

"When are we leaving?" the three friends asked in unison.

"You can't possibly think I'm going to take the three of you," C.J. said in a dismissing tone and moved toward Nick. "I have to leave now. Hand over the computer, Nick, and leave the Ladder program running."

Nick backed toward the door and bumped into a military officer. "Hand over the computer or I'll be forced to use extreme measures," Nick quickly transferred the computer to C.J. "Are you ready to go sir? Your transport is waiting on the roof."

"I'm ready. You should find the Ladder program running lock onto their coordinates, but first we have to pick up Detective Michaels."

The two men left the room and Jamie tried to run after them, Chief McGovens grabbed her arm. "No Jamie, it has to be done this way. If I had a choice I would be right there with them," He pulled her into a fatherly hug while she calmed down. "Let's go call your father. He'll want to know your okay and could you take care of the officer Niles injured." She gave him a forced smile.

"Sir, what is it with those kids?" The officer inquired and prepared for take-off.

"Their friend is right in the middle of this mess. That is a great bunch of minds back there. I wish I had such loyal friends growing up." He remembered his sheltered childhood. He had little interaction with kids his own age, from the age of three he has lived on Plutonus. The government took him away from his home and put him through rigorous testing, trained him to focus his physic abilities, now the government used him to interrogate suspects. At first the headaches were mild, but over the years they have steadily increased. I wonder if Jamie will teach me how to use her herbal medicines. He was shaken from his thoughts with the officer's announcement.

"We're almost at the farm, sir."

Detective Michaels was standing on the side of the road impatiently waiting. He was carrying a bag loaded with supplies including the latest arsenal and explosives. The transport landed only long enough to pick him up. They were zooming through the air and were out of the atmosphere before Kane realized it. "Where do you think they're headed?"

"They can't get far. Their supply transport will be picked up shortly by a larger transporter. We'll catch up with them there."

Robert nudged Sam awake when they reached space. "Take a look around."

Sam was now staring out the window at all the stars and couldn't believe her eyes. There were a number of transport ships of all shapes and sizes and the air looked so clean. Pretoria had a greenish glow haloing the planet proclaiming it toxic free. She wondered if the first settlers were in awe as she was now.

"Have you ever seen so many beautiful stars? What's that over there?" He shook his head forgetting Sam had never left Pretoria until today. He attempted to answer all her questions when the largest transporter came into sight. He stopped her question and pointed to the large object just outside the window.

"That is how we are going to get to Plutonus. Just keep watching out the window and you will see more than you ever dreamed." Robert settled back to listen to the pilot's transmission and heard exactly what he wanted.

"We have two unauthorized passengers trying to intercept a diplomatic pouch. Please have military officers at landing bay for apprehension and questioning."

"Roger that. Assistance will be awaiting your arrival. You are green to land at bay tango alpha."

"Copy that."

There was a slight jerk when the supply transport landed. "Come on you two." Matthew waved his weapon in a shoeing gesture.

"Sam, stay close," he whispered to her.

"No problem." She grabbed his hand and got as close as she possible could.

The transport door was yanked from Ms. Johnson's grasp as in rushed multiple military officers. "Drop your weapons!"

They dropped their weapons and were searched. He proceeded to tell the officer in charge, "We work for Chancellor Hilary Lansing. We were caring a diplomatic pouch and these two tried to steal it." He pointed in their direction.

"Could I see your credentials?" the officer asked Mr. Matthew and Ms. Johnson. He couldn't take his eyes off the young woman dressed in a skintight black outfit, standing next to the imposingly dressed man with a military air.

"Of course. Here are our papers." He handed the officer a packet of information.

"We have to radio and verify these, until then we have to hold all of you." Sam was nervous over the display before her and squeezed his hand tighter.

He stepped forward releasing her hand and was surrounded by officers. "I can solve this faster."

"Okay, how?" The officers looked at him with skepticism, he was still dressed in fatigues a blood soaked bandage on his left bicep added the air of danger he presented.

He reached down slowly uncovering his military tattoo. He proceeded to tell the officers he had been ordered to apprehend Mr. Matthew and Ms. Johnson for treason among other things. "I need to radio Christopher Jackknife. I believe he should be arriving any minute. He'll verify my identity and Miss Sam Gabriels.

"Please extend your wrist," The officer pulled out a blue wand and scanned the information tattooed there. He looked down at the information immediately stood at attention and saluted. "This will do fine. Welcome back Colonel Michaels."

There was a commotion at the bay entrance where C.J. and Kane had been trying to gain entry. Sam was still trying to absorb everything she had learned. She saw Kane and C.J. extend their arms and an officer scan them.

"Thank you. Here is Christopher now. He should have arrest

warrants for one Barnabas Matthew and one Francis Johnson."

"Colonel Michaels, I believe you are waiting on these. Sorry it took so long three others wanted to join us." He smiled slightly as he presented Robert with the warrants.

Robert turned to officer in charge, "I believe these are the papers you need."

Francis Johnson started to struggle as the officers restrained her. "They're lying! They're the ones suspected of treason."

"Shut up Francis. This is your entire fault." Matthew yelled as she got a dumbfounded look. They were then taken holding cells to await questioning.

Sam sighed in relief when she saw Detective Michaels familiar face even if her friends couldn't be here she knew she had one ally.

CHAPTER 18

THE OFFICER in charge motioned to one of his lieutenants and had a brief conversation with him. "If you follow my Lieutenant, Colonel, I believe we have suitable accommodations for you and your companions." He eyed Sam until Robert stepped in front of her. They left the landing bay surrounded by armed officers and entered the main hallway.

There was a lot to absorb on the transport station. Sam was having difficulty taking in everything she saw, and Jamie would want details. She checked out the surroundings. There were shops, restaurants, theaters, and office fronts. She edged closer to Robert and he reached down to take her hand. People turned to stare at the group being escorted by military police. C.J. and Kane took up positions around her. C.J. moved to her right, Robert stayed to her left, and Kane followed close behind. The three men towered over Sam's five-foot-five thin frame.

They were escorted directly to a suite of rooms. Sam was relieved to be away from all the prying eyes. She was able to retrieve her bag before leaving the docking bay and left to take a hot shower. The three men sat down at the table to discuss strategy. She shut and locked the door and faced herself in the mirror. Sam shook her head at her appearance and turned on the shower. No wonder the officers were staring at her. She'd only had a few minutes to shower that morning and the only clothes she'd had were her emergency gear. Her outfit consisted of a black pair of skintight pants, matching top, black shoes, and a cap. The outfit was designed for ease of movement no matter what situation she found herself in.

Standing in the pulsing spray of the shower Sam had time to think about the events of the past few days. She finally gave way to frustration and fear, and slipped to the floor of the tub and cried until she was spent. She was trained to be a warrior and show no emotion while on a mission. "Never let them see your fear, never let them see your fatigue, and never let them see you when you're down," her father's words echoed in her mind. Sam went over all the conversations she'd over heard. She stopped and replayed, then looked down at her arm where Robert had grabbed her the day before. There was a small red mark. She became angry and quickly finished her shower. Grabbing a robe, she pulled open the door to confront Robert.

The three men looked up at the sound of the bathroom door opening. Sam stormed across the floor and pointed a finger at Robert. "How could you tag me? Is there no such thing as privacy anymore? I trusted you. It's bad enough someone else has been following me for the past year. Then they have Mattie pushed into my inner circle."

"What does she mean?" C.J. asked of Robert.

"I'll tell you. The cell knows who my friends are and where we hang out. I haven't been to that farm in over a year. Tell me how they knew that if they haven't been following me!" Sam began her familiar pacing.

"Sam, it was necessary that I put a trace on you, I lost sight of you twice in one day. I had to be sure that disk made it into the right hands." He took her by the shoulders and turned her toward himself. He could see the fire in her eyes. He removed his hands quickly. "I did it to protect you and your father."

Sam kept eye contact with him as the tears began to flow. Her hatred was so strong that the tears felt like acid. "Did you also hear our conversations? And what's this about you being a Colonel? You sure didn't need my help or that of my friends' to rescue my dad, let alone identify the cell members' real names. Does my father know who you really are?"

"Yes, I admit I heard everything you and your friends said. I had to know what you were up to. I had to lead you to believe I was just another operative until I could trust you. Your father didn't know until we rescued him that I was working for M.I. I needed your help identifying the cell members. Besides, the government doesn't have the kind of software Nick has developed."

Sam wiped the tears away with the back of her hand and began to shake. C.J. sensed something was changing, so he watched the couple. Then it happened. Standing in front of Robert was an exact copy of him.

"What the hell?" Kane tried to move to his feet and C.J. placed a restraining hand on his arm, holding him firmly in place.

"Don't do anything to interrupt her concentration. This is fascinating."

Robert couldn't move—he was still stunned at the vision in front of him it was like looking in a mirror. He said in a low voice, "Sam?" She broke eye contact and changed back to her normal form. Robert took a firm hold on her as she slid to the floor. He scooped her up and placed her gently on the bed. He then turned to C.J. "Can you explain what happened and why it hasn't happened before?"

"I can explain only part of it. She's supposed to be classified as a mimic. Apparently she or someone else has been suppressing it. It was not mentioned in her file, but after meeting Nick, Niles, and Jamie, I'm not surprised. I do remember reading that her mother is a botanist. She could be placing something in Sam's food. She is the first true mimic I've met."

"I'm trying to understand. She can change into anyone she sees?" Kane had moved closer to Sam who was now sleeping.

"From what I've read, your assumption is correct, Kane."

"No wonder her parents suppressed it. The government or someone else would find her very valuable."

"She could've ended up like me," C.J. made his decision to protect Sam at all costs. "We have to keep this information to ourselves." The three men agreed with a nod.

Robert took a seat next to Sam on the bed and moved a lock of her hair that had fallen in her face. "I've met a mimic only once before, but not with her skill. The mimic I met couldn't hold his shape for long and there was always some deformity. Will she be okay?" He inquired of C.J. with out looking away from her.

"She will, but I'll take a look around just to make sure." He proceeded to read Sam's mind and discovered her earliest memories of changing identities. A smile grew across his face at the normal childhood her parents tried to give her.

"Well? Did you find anything out?" Kane asked when he saw C.J. open his eyes.

"Give me a minute," He rubbed a hand over his temples and popped a few pills into his mouth. "Wish Jamie was here with her bag of tricks. From the time she was four she would mimic the postman, her parents, and an older lady. It was pretty funny seeing a miniature Aron. She's going to be okay, but her parents have been suppressing her gift for so long, I'm afraid Sam has forgotten how to use and control it."

With concern in his voice Robert asked the question that was bothering him. "When do you think she'll wake up?"

"In a couple of hours. She's been through quite a trauma. I'm going to do some research. We may be able to use this gift to our advantage."

"Not if it's going to harm her. I won't let you do it." He spun around to look C.J. in the face and looked as mad as a wounded wolf.

"Neither will I. I've come to think of Sam as a sister," Kane said. The two cousins gave identical fierce looks in C.J.'s direction.

He had his hands up in surrender. "If I find out that it'll harm her in any way, we won't do it."

Kane moved to sit on the other side of Sam. "Aron will kill us if anything happens to her."

"Aron may not be the one to worry about. I have a feeling three others would want first crack at us," They shared a smile, thinking of the three friends back on Pretoria. "We should call her father."

"Good idea. He could tell me more than some textbook. Leave it to me." C.J. went into the other bedroom closing the door for privacy.

Kane got up from the bed. "I'm going for a bite to eat. Want me to bring you anything?"

"Yes, and bring something for Sam for when she wakes up." Robert didn't even look up. He kept his eyes on Sam.

Kane left the room and couldn't believe the change in his cousin. When did he turn soft? He used to be so hard and untouchable. nothing and no one could penetrate his armor. Leave it to a red head with emerald eyes to enchant his cousin, the solider. *That'll never happen to me,* he vowed.

In the hospital emergency room Annie Gabriels was being examined. She had a broken arm and some minor abrasions. Aron was on the phone with his staff arranging for a diplomat to met Sam on Plutonus with credentials. He hung up the phone and turned to Annie. "Everything has been arranged. I wish I knew how things are going up there. I trust Robert and Kane is close behind. Sam should be alright, I trained her the best I could."

He looked at Annie, saw the tears on her face, and went to comfort her. "Our daughter is strong. She can take care of herself. She's always done what we told her, even when she didn't want to. Remember that time she changed in to Patrick's mother and scared her half to death? Sam didn't want to change back because she was having fun bossing Nick and Niles around."

Annie remembered, and then became somber once more. "Aron, she's never left the planet before and she hasn't been home to eat in a long time. At some point she's going to change. I just hope she's not alone. We've been suppressing her gift for so long that I'm not sure how she'll react. She's fit physically, but emotionally she'll be unstable. What are we going to do if the government finds out?"

"When the time comes, it may not matter. When I started the alliance, it was to make the government sit up and take notice. The planet of Pretoria needs its people treated equally, not sheltered and shuttled away. I'm afraid the cell has made it more difficult for us and our plight," Aron's satellite phone rang. He looked down and saw C.J. was calling. He answered in a panic. "C.J., has something happened? Is Sam alright?"

"Something has happened, but let me assure you that she's going to be fine. Are you in a secure location? We have a few important things to discuss," he replied calmly.

"Annie and I are still at the hospital. We're in a clean room set aside for diplomats." Annie was watching Aron and having a hard time staying away from the phone. She wanted to know if her daughter was okay.

"First, Kane and I made it in time, but Robert already had the situation under control. Did you know he was a Colonel?"

"Not until the other day, but that doesn't matter. I knew he served."

"Mr. Matthew and Ms. Johnson are in custody waiting for me to interrogate them before we reach Plutonus," He waited a beat then came right out and asked, "How long has Sam been a mimic?"

Aron's head dropped forward and he rubbed a hand over his furrowed brow. "Since she was two. How did you find out? She wasn't in public was she?"

C.J. laughed. "She and Robert were arguing they were in our room. Sam finally figured out Robert had her tagged and that he was a Colonel. All the sudden she changed into Robert, but not for long. She's weak and sleeping at the moment. I checked her out and found her earliest memories. How have you been suppressing her gift?"

"Annie, with the help of Jamie's grandmother, mixed a plant ingredient to her morning food. She was worried this might happen." Aron glanced over to his wife and took her hand in his.

"How powerful is her gift? I noticed she only held Robert's shape for a little bit."

"She's out of practice. We've been suppressing her gift for over fifteen years. If she concentrates she can hold a shape for up to two hours, maybe longer. It depends on her state of mind. When she is really concentrating, nothing can stop her. That's why we suppressed it. Annie was afraid the government would take her away and use her. She couldn't bear to be separated from her only child." After Jamie's mother left, she promised to protect both girls should they develop a gift.

"How long will it be before Sam can use her gift to full capacity?" C.J. jotted down some notes while he listened.

Aron asked his wife and she shook her head. "I don't want her to use her gift."

"Annie, please tell me. Please? Think of our daughter's safety," He squeezed her hand. "They need to know the truth to protect her."

"The suppression should completely wear off in about four hours by my calculations." Annie couldn't help worrying, her baby was exposed and two people who worked for M.I. knew. Based on planetary law they could be punished if it was found out.

"Did you hear that, C.J.?" He squeezed Annie's free hand.

"I did. What can we do to help her redevelop her gift?" he asked cautiously.

"Hand her photos and have her concentrate. Start out with simple similar body and facial profiles, and then increase the difficulty," Aron answered, remembering the numerous tests they tried when Sam first developed the gift.

"I have one more question. How were you able to keep it out of her file?" There was silence for a moment.

"We were able to find out before they started testing. I have arranged credentials and a diplomat will be waiting when you land on Plutonus. Promise to take good care of my girl."

"I don't think that will be a problem. Robert and Kane haven't left her side since we left the landing bay. They know there are a few people who will be very upset if Sam were to be hurt. I'll keep you updated. You have a very special young woman here, sir."

Aron hung up and relayed the conversation to Annie. Her mood had lightened and there was a mischievous look in her eye. "I wonder if there was more going on than we know about? I hope my suspicions are right. How soon can we go home, Aron?"

With a sigh Aron said, "We won't be going home just yet. We're being taken to a government safe house until things are settled and the leader of the cell is captured."

CHAPTER 19

NICK, NILES, and Jamie were escorted to an apartment above the police department that was used by government officials. The apartment had top-notch security and was swept for bugs on a weekly basis. There were three bedrooms, two separate baths, and a kitchen and dinning area.

"Jamie, I want you to call your father. Let him know where you are and that you'll be staying here for a while."

"Okay, Mr. McGovens. Can I have him bring me some things?" She took a look at her day emergency clothes. They were the same as Sam's.

"Whatever you think you're going to need for at least the next forty-eight hours. Have him bring it to my office. All of you try and get some rest. If Aron or Kane call I'll fill you in. There's food in the fridge, so help yourselves. Whatever you do, do not leave this apartment. Apparently the cell knows who you are, which put you at risk. Niles, you and I will talk later about your actions." Chief McGovens left, posting two fresh officers outside the door. If they wanted past the guards, they wouldn't be able to stop them. Aron had trained them well—his officers were still reeling. Niles had done a number on his officer's wrist and hand. He'd be lucky if the officer didn't press charges against Niles.

His father came to him, adamant that Aron be allowed to train them at a young age. He said their survival would depend on their training and dedication. He would be pleased with their progress. His mother mentioned it was Sam's time. He always asked the boys what story their grandfather had told them that evening. They would never tell him. Niles mentioned that grandpa said the stories were for them to remember. He questioned his father once about Niles' answer and he said in good time they would be revealed. Patrick wandered down to his office to pull old cases and mark them solved, five years he'd waited for just this opportunity.

Nick moved to the desk while Jamie called her dad. He set up his computer system and opened his security program alpha and logged easily into Barnabas Matthew's computer system. He found the files marked deliveries to Plutonus and saw a number of diplomatic pouches returning to one specific name, Chancellor Hilary Lansing. Nick was able to obtain information that each pouch contained a list of supplies, funds, and several other documents. He left Matthew's computer through the back door, erasing any evidence that he was there.

Next he moved to the government computer on Plutonus, Nick knew that what he was doing was illegal. His father would want to talk to him, too. They had to find out what was going on before Sam reached Plutonus. Niles walked up behind him and saw the print out. He took the print out to the table to study the information.

Hours later, they had eaten a light meal, changed, and Jamie's dad had left. Jamie moved to the window to watch the sunset. She was staring, deep in thought, wishing they could've gone with them—another adventure to a strange world. *The different plants and herbs I could have found, the possibilities are endless,* Jamie thought. Sam seemed to have all the fun. Jamie remembered an early memory or maybe it was a dream that Sam could change identities, It was probable just a dream.

Over the years they had a lot of misadventures, many in Sam's house or on the McGovens farm. Sam had taken her into the pantry one day and showed her the hidden room. When they were caught, Sam asked her father if Jamie could learn with her . . . then the twins had to learn. Her father agreed, but only after a lot of begging and a talk with grandpa McGovens. Jamie would never forget the lessons she learned from Aron Gabriels. Jamie was pulled from her musing when Niles groaned. "What is it, Niles?"

"This is getting messy. This information Nick found on Matthew's computer implicates an official high up in Plutonus government. There are only four people on Plutonus that receive diplomatic pouches from Pretoria and one of them is Chancellor Hilary Lansing listed here."

"I've been trying to check out that name I found with those files, but I'm having a problem getting past the firewall. I started running my omega security program before we ate and it still hasn't found the correct password," Nick looked at his friends "Any suggestions?"

"Have you tried all the common passwords?" Niles inquired, still matching dates on the papers before him. His mind was working furiously. All the data was adding up to a very big political downfall that would change Pretoria forever.

"I started with those first. No luck. Jamie, have any ideas?"

"Are we talking woman, right?" She tapped a finger to her lips in thought.

"What does that matter?" Niles frowned at Jamie and rubbed a hand across his brow.

"It actually matters a lot. A man would not use a cats name for example." Nick got to thinking that maybe it could be that simple. He returned to his computer and did a general Internet search on the suspect, Hilary Lansing. He never thought to try a cat's name, and there it was—a picture with her big fluffy white cat with blue eyes. He tried childhood nicknames, birthdates, identification numbers, and other drivel. He stopped the omega program and entered her cat's name "Phobia." His computer started to spill out data and his eyes grew large at the information. He had to wipe his hands on his jeans they were sweating so badly. He was in deep and wasn't liking what he found. He'd wondered why Robert and Kane kept saying the city had eyes now he knew why.

Nick started to do a file-by-file search for any mention of Matthew, Johnson, or Weston. He knew they needed hard evidence to nail her. Niles and Jamie were huddled in conversation when Nick found what he was looking for and it wasn't hidden very well. Nick stopped typing and the printer stopped printing. A hush fell over the room only to be broken by the knock on the door signaling Aron and Patrick's arrival with Annie. He quickly exited the system and logged off. Dad was going to be mad enough.

Aron and Patrick noticed the print outs scattered on the table. They picked up a few and scanned the contents. Patrick asked, "Where did you get this information?" He put a hand up in a stopping motion when Nick went to speak. "No, wait . . . don't tell me." Aron noticed another stack of papers on the printer. He walked over and picked up the top sheet to read. He just didn't believe what he was holding. A very high government official was the head of the cell and they had hard evidence to confirm that information.

"Mr. Gabriels, what are you doing here?" Jamie said asked with a note of fear in her voice.

"It was decided that we should stay together. I've talked to C.J. and have some information for you. It looks like you have some information to share too." Aron was still perusing the data in his hand. He laid it down, gathered more of the papers, and skimmed over them. A frown marred his features as he reviewed the last pile.

Niles mouth had gone dry and he took a sip of soda. "Sam's alright? Nothing bad has happened?" Jamie grabbed his hand and squeezed and Nick sat down next to her taking her other hand. Unity they had been taught was the key to any successful team. Rarely did they let outsiders inside the group. The bond the four of them had was strong they seemed to compliment one another.

Aron turned around and faced Sam's friends then looked at his wife to make sure she was in agreement. Annie nodded and he took a seat on the sofa across from them. "First, I'll tell you everything went well. They reached the transport carrier safely and met with resistance. Robert explained the situation and presented his credentials—the tables were turned. Mr. Matthew and Ms. Johnson are in custody waiting for C.J. to do his job." There was a collective sigh of relief around the room.

"What kind of credentials? I thought Robert was just an operative?" Niles asked confused about the information then remembered the tattoo he'd glimpsed.

"You know him as Robert Michaels, but in reality he is Colonel Robert Michaels, M.I. Special Forces division. He was recruited to infiltrate the alliance and find out who was causing the problem." There was a collective gasp around the room no one knew what to say.

"There are things you may not remember about Sam. You were all so young when it happened," Annie seized his hand. "Since she was two years old we knew she had a special talent. She is classified as a mimic and can change into anyone, including your grandmother." He looked at Nick and Niles. "Do you remember that day Sam disappeared and your grandmother appeared?"

Niles eyes opened wide. "I remember that day. Grandma was supposed to be in town shopping and Mrs. Gabriels was watching us. She made us give her all those kisses, and I thought something was funny."

"I thought that was a dream," Jamie replied, her thought from earlier rushing back.

"Since that day, Annie and I have been suppressing her gift by natural ingredients with your grandmothers help, Jamie. As you can see, we have a problem. Sam hasn't been home in days. She changed in front of C.J., Kane, and Robert. The suppression will wear off in a couple of hours and Sam will have full use of her gift." Annie shivered.

"Grandma McGovens knew about Sam. Before I left for the house she told me to tell Sam to remember her strengths," Nick gave a hardy laugh. "Probably gave her heart palpations to see Sam like that."

"It sure did. Your grandmother will never forget that day." Patrick joined Nick, holding a hand to his stomach as it shook.

Aron held up a stack of papers and the laughing abruptly stopped. "What is all this data and don't tell me where you obtained it," Aron captured the looks of the three conspirators and focused on Niles.

Niles separated the papers into three piles. He gathered the first pile and handed it to Aron. "This pile here is a copy of the diplomatic pouches returned to Plutonus via Mr. Matthew's office. The dates match murders, sabotage, and supply thefts. I've taken the liberty of correlating names and dates going back five years," He handed that pile to his father. "This pile contains files pertaining to the exact information of each diplomatic pouch. Included you will find dates, times, and operatives involved," Niles picked up the last pile and cautiously handed it to Aron. "This last pile includes memos concerning legislation here on Pretoria."

The room became so quiet you could hear a pin drop. Nick cleared his throat. "Sir, are you angry with us? I know it's not legal . . . how we attended the information. We were trying to help."

"No, I'm not mad. I could have used you three years ago. We might not be in this mess today. I am curious about this legislation you mentioned, Niles. Can you summarize it for me?" Aron perused the papers while Niles explained the basics.

"The legislation, if passed, would mean the citizens of Pretoria would have no voting rights in major government elections. Citizens of Pretoria would only be able to vote on a city level. There was also bill attached to it that would allow a person to own slaves specifically the gifted. Isn't that a little harsh, Mr. Gabriels?"

"Yes. That's why we have to stop this as soon as possible. It also explains why Sam was being watched, someone found out about her gift. They are going to use us as an example." Aron looked at his wife who had been quite. He wondered how they would survive without Sam.

Aron walked over to the desk and dialed C.J.'s satellite phone, and within a minute the connection was made. "Hello, C.J. How is my daughter doing?"

"She's feeling much better. Do you need to speak with her?" He gave a rare smile when he saw Sam change into the latest male pop star. Kane went out earlier at her urging and picked up a few popular magazines.

"Actually, I called to talk to you. I have some new information on the leader of the cell and it changes how she has to be approached."

"Did you say *she*? Who is this person?" He slipped back into the other room.

"Hilary Lansing, Chancellor of Interplanetary Affairs. I have evidence in my hand that implicates her in all activity for the past five years. She was also trying to pass legislation to more or less turn Pretoria into a slave colony and take away the voting rights from the citizens. She needs to be stopped."

"Mr. Gabriels are you sure this information is accurate?" C.J. asked in stunned belief. He'd worked with Chancellor Lansing once before and hadn't sensed anything unusual. He was younger and less experienced.

"The evidence came directly from Barnabas Matthew and Chancellor Lansing's computers," Aron stated matter of factly.

"Looks like I need to get to work before we reach Plutonus. I'll have Robert contact his commander," C.J. rubbed his temples thinking of the headache he was going to have.

He turned around to face the trio practicing Sam's gift. He was amazed by the progress she had made in such a short time. She had moved from holding an image only a few seconds to fifteen minutes with little concentration or thought. He hated to break up the fun, but work came first. "You're getting pretty good at that, but we've had a few new developments."

Sam changed back and frowned up at him. "Has something happened to my parents or my friends?"

He was quick to reassure her that that wasn't the case. "They're just fine. Your friends have been very busy. They found interesting information on Barnabas Matthew's computer and a certain high-ranking official's computer. There were memos regarding legislation that if passed will take voting rights away from Pretoria. If that were to happen, you and our kind would be in danger. Robert, you should report into your commander and get him up to date. I need to head down to interrogation and confirm some information," He faced Sam and hesitated to ask his next question. "Sam, we may need your help. Do you feel up to it?" If he couldn't get them to cooperate in the usually way, maybe Sam could confront them with the very person they feared.

Robert and Kane were watching Sam's reaction while holding their breaths. She quickly changed into C.J. "What do you think?" She grinned up at him when she changed back.

"I guess I have my answer. I'm off to talk to Mr. Matthew." He was halted by Robert. He looked directly at him. "You need to know who this official is, right?"

"You got that right! Don't try to hedge either." Robert's face was a blank mask, C.J. felt his anger, he didn't have to see it.

"Hilary Lansing, Chancellor of Interplanetary Affairs." C.J. answered calmly as he left the room.

Robert stunned by the announcement, grabbed his phone to contact his commander. "Chancellor Ronin? Colonel Michaels reporting in. There have been major developments over the last seventy-two hours."

"I am aware of the developments on Pretoria. I understand you are currently on a transport carrier to Plutonus. There are two prisoners and the mayor's daughter," Chancellor Ronin stated.

"The prisoners are cell members Barnabas Matthew and Francis Johnson. Circumstances forced the mayor's daughter to join me. Sir, I have evidence that Hilary Lansing is leading the cell. How do you wish me to proceed?" There was a silent pause before he answered.

"You have your orders Colonel Michaels. Proceed as planned. This mission cannot fail."

"Yes, sir, I understand my mission." Robert hung up the phone, fell into a seat, and ran his hands through his hair. He laid his elbows to rest on his thighs and bowed his head in thought.

Sam moved from the bed and kneeled before Robert trying to see his face. "What's the matter? Look at me and tell me who you talked to?"

He jiggled his head and got up to pace, he needed time to think. *How can he complete this mission?* He wondered. *He'd be assassinating a Chancellor. How in the world could he get close enough to finish this job? I can't do this at her office, I don't want to risk anyone else going in there, and security was extremely tight. He'd need Nick's help with the layout and security schedule of her mansion. Kane could devise a distraction if he needed one. He couldn't believe his orders stood to take out the source of the cell and eliminate anyone who interferes.*

Sam stepped in front of Robert. He was so deep in thought that he ran into her. He grabbed her shoulders before she fell. "Now, tell me." Robert's eyes had turned cold and Sam took a step back.

He looked at Kane with a frown. "My orders stand, there is to be no deviation. I'm going to need your help. Are you up for it?" His voice was even colder and sent a shiver down her spine.

Kane stared at him with open-mouthed astonishment. "You have to take out the Chancellor?"

"Those are my orders. I have to assassinate the Chancellor."

"Damn," Kane plopped down on the bed and put his hand over his eyes. "How do you plan to accomplish this mission?"

"I'm still working out the details," He finally looked down at Sam and saw the fear he put there and made his decision. He was the one to involve her. If it wasn't for that disk, she'd be safe at home. He had to complete his mission if only for her safety. "Sweetheart, call Nick. I need his help," He leaned down and kissed her gently holding her tight knowing they had little time left. He leaned back and saw the unanswered questions. Now was not the time for answers. Any relationship he would want to start with her would have to wait. They had this odd chemistry passing between them and he wanted to explore more of it. Unfortunately, they might not get the chance.

How could this guys kisses tie her in knots so quickly? At times it feels like she'd known him forever, she wondered. His hard edge and cool demeanor told nothing about the man she was beginning to love. Could it truly be love on a grand scale or just a passing infatuation? He was going to protect her at all costs, that she was sure of and left no doubt. Things may turn out differently once his mission was completed. She'd help him in any way she could, even if it meant going against his demands.

Sam didn't hesitate when Robert handed her the phone. After two rings Nick answered. "Hello?"

"Hey, Nick. How are things going?" She tried to sound cheerful, but it was a performance she couldn't fake. Her friends knew her to well.

Nick was literally thrown off the couch when he heard Sam's voice and it took him a minute to get his bearings. "Sam. Are you really okay? Your dad told us about your gift and we were able to give him the name of the cell leader." Jamie and Niles had gathered close to hear the conversation.

"I'm okay. Robert needs our help. I'm not sure what he needs so I'll let you talk to him." She handed the phone over and moved away.

"Nick, do you think you can get me a layout for the Chancellor's home and see if you can't get a copy of the security detail? E-mail them to me, you know the address." When Nick went to interrupt he cut him off. "Please don't ask any questions you'll be debriefed later."

"It may take some doing, but sure whatever you need. Can we talk to Sam again?" He asked shyly, not sure if Robert would let him. There was something cold in his voice.

Robert passed back the phone to Sam. "Don't be long."

Jamie snatched the phone from Nick and received two nasty identical looks. "How are you really doing, Sam?" Jamie slapped Niles hand away from the phone and moved toward the window seat.

Sam laughed at Jamie's serious tone. "At first it was a little scary being held at gun point, and then the transport was stormed. I moved about in a daze till everything hit me and when I realized Robert had tagged me, I broke down. This weird thing happened and now I'm having some fun. I suppose my parents filled you in. Things are changing so fast, I want to tell you everything, but

Robert said I have to keep it short." He was currently glaring at her from across the room. She glared right back in defiance.

"I'm glad to hear everything is okay. Be careful and come home soon. Nick and Niles are driving me nuts," Jamie sounded exasperated and caused Sam to laugh.

Sam could just picture what Jamie was going through. There were times her mom watched the twins and they would be fighting for her notice. "Look you have the undivided attention of two very good looking guys. You can't beat that," Kane gave Sam a furious look. "I'll see you soon, Jamie. Hang in there."

"You hang in there, too. We miss you Sam."

CHAPTER 20

C.J. entered the interrogation room where two armed military officers were waiting with Francis Johnson. She looked up when he entered the room with fire in her eyes. She had dark shadows under her eyes and her hair and clothes were disheveled. She spit out, "I have nothing to tell you. Matthew is the one. It's entirely his fault. I never wanted anything to do with this mess."

He calmly took a seat across from her. "I will be the judge of that." He proceeded to read her mind and found she believed the government was ordering the events they have committed. In one memory he saw her shoot several people with no remorse. In another he saw her hand over the diplomatic pouches to Lynn Weston joking about the next target. She gave him nothing new, only Hilary's name again which was mentioned in conversation with Matthews. He left the room felling nauseous then ordered the officers to take her away and bring Barnabas Matthew. He leaned against the wall popped some more pills, closed his eyes, and willed his headache away.

He should have asked Jamie for her headache remedy. If he didn't think they would be a risk, he would've brought her friends. They each had a special talent that could be valuable to their current mission. Past experience reminded him what would happen if they government got wind of their uniqueness. It was bad enough they were risking Sam's exposure.

A little while later, Barnabas Matthew was escorted into the room and cuffed to the chair across from C.J. "Are you willing to talk?" he asked in his coldest tone.

"Why would I?" Barnabas spewed out at C.J. Matthew's normally perfect appearance was in total disarray. "I gave you a choice, remember?" C.J. commenced his scan and faced resistance on Matthew's part. He finally broke through and saw him receiving orders from Chancellor Lansing to have Sam followed. He was to contact her teachers, neighbors, local officers, and Mattie Grant. They were to keep a close eye on her and watch for any change. He saw Mattie was put in place after they discovered Ms. Weston's disk. Next, he saw the brutal assassination of the Provincial Governor of Mantis by the supposed witness and Lynn Weston wiping his mind. It was believed that Robert gave the disk to the governor, in an effort to recover the disk he was eliminated. Matthew was under the assumption that the governor was the leader of the alliance, not Aron Gabriels.

C.J. saw a discussion with Chancellor Lansing. The conversation was about her future plans. She was adamant to push legislation to abolish voting rights on Pretoria. Once the law was passed, as Interplanetary Chancellor, she would be able to take over the planet and use all gifted citizens to her advantage. They would be forced into her service.

Lastly, he saw Chancellor Lansing order Matthews to deliver the disk to her personally and eliminate anyone who got in the way. He completed his scan and almost collapsed from the stress of maintaining contact his nose started to bleed. Barnabas Matthew had passed out and C.J. had the officers take him to the medical clinic. "Remember to keep him well guarded."

He staggered his way back to the room and promptly fell on the bed and went to sleep. His last thought was *He really didn't want to do this anymore, time for a new career.*

Robert was pouring over the e-mail from Nick with extreme concentration. Kane was taking a nap, C.J. was still passed out from his latest interrogation and Sam was getting restless. She was furiously flipping through the magazines Kane brought back and threw them down in frustration. "I need to get out of this room. How long before we reach Plutonus anyway?"

Robert looked up from the computer only long enough to respond. "We'll arrive in about four more hours. Now, sit down and quit pacing. You're distracting me." Sam walked over to claim a few items from her travel bag and attempted to leave the room. He was quicker and reached the door first leaning against it. "Where do you think your going?"

"I'm going exploring and I could use a change of clothes. Move aside or I'll have to hurt you." Sam was really getting annoyed by his over possessiveness and had to get out. She moved forward another step and was inches away from him.

"Sweetheart, you couldn't hurt me," His smile reached all the way to his eyes. She put a hand to his wrist stroked it and smiled up at him. The next thing he knew he was flat on his back gasping for air. He quickly rolled over, grabbed her ankle and pulled her toward him. "You think it's that easy to take me down?" He growled at her, swiftly standing up while holding her ankle. Sam took the opportunity to get in a good round kick hitting him in the jaw. In the next instant she found herself suspended in mid air by her ankles in his unrelenting grip. "Sam, stop this. I don't want to hurt you."

"Let me go. You do know I have other moves up my sleeve and you're in a vulnerable position." She proceeded to show him by pinching the backside of his knee causing him to buckle and come crashing down. He tossed her over his back with her legs locked in his arms ready for her next move. Sam gave up, knowing she was out manned this time, but kept her hands bunched in a fist. Breathing hard now she was trying to get her second wind when he tossed her to the floor the force knocked the breath from her. "Okay, I give." Robert sagged down next to her rubbing the back of his knee.

When he caught his breath he asked, "Did your father teach you that?"

"Yes, every day for two hours since I was five. We have a gym set up in the house." Sam was still catching her breath as she answered and rubbed her ribs.

He glared at her, searching his memory for an unidentified room. "I never saw a gym and I searched that whole house."

She gave him a grin and stretched out loosening her muscles that began to cramp. She really needed a good workout. "There's an entrance in the pantry blocked by shelves. The entrance has a very sophisticated security program involving thumb print and retina verification."

Kane had moved over to the two on the floor. "Have you two had enough? I agree, she needs to get out of this room. I'll go with her and show her the sights." He said with a grin only for Sam, knowing it would get his cousins goat. Robert swept his foot in a quick motion and knocked him to the floor. He looked at Kane's know-it-all face and knew he was beat. Kane looked at Sam with amusement and just knew his cousin would give in to her demands.

"She can go," Sam started to get up, he grabbed her hand and she was forced to face him, "But I'm coming, too. I could use a break. We'll let C.J. sleep in peace maybe he'll be awake when we get back." The trio left the room to explore the many shops on the transport. Following not far behind were the two officers assigned to protect Sam.

They entered the main transport area and Sam stopped and did a slow turn. Where to start first? There was so much to choose from. She was brought out of her thoughts by Robert's warm breath on her cheek. "Where would you like to go first?" She swallowed hard and pointed to an upscale clothing shop with short skirts and skimpy tops in the window.

She looked up at Robert with a sparkle in her eyes. "That's where we start." She tugged on his hand and Kane laughed following along. He was looking forward to watching his cousin squirm.

After seven stores, one restaurant and a mound of bags the trio returned and C.J. was waiting for them drinking a cup of coffee. "There you are. Did you enjoy yourselves?" He couldn't believe the amount of bags Kane and Robert were carrying and grinned at the spectacle.

Kane was glad to see C.J. up and about he looked awful when he returned from interrogation. He had slept for hours and still looked pale as a ghost. He could still see the dark circles under his eyes. If only Jamie were here she could have helped bring C.J. back to normal. Kane remembered how she helped with Lynn Weston; they never would have gotten this far with out that truth serum. Kane placed the bags on the bed and grabbed a cup of coffee joining him at the table.

Robert followed Sam in and dropped his bags inside the door. He turned around with a mocking smile. "If you think it's so funny you should go with her next time." Sam slapped him on the back. He flinched, turned around and grabbed her wrist, and hauled her up against him. He smiled down at Sam and said, "I was just kidding. It was rather fun. I never knew someone who could change so fast and cover so much ground in that little time," He looked over his shoulder at Kane and grinned. "We should recruit her."

"We should. With that temperament, those quick moves, and evasiveness she's a natural," Kane lifted his cup in a toast. "Is Jamie that good? The government is always looking for women."

Sam relaxed at the easy banter and played along. She batted her lashes. "When do I start my training? Jamie is as good as I am, if not better. She also trained with my father." Robert looked down at her, eased his grip, and rubbed the spot with his thumb. Sam backed away at the intimate contact and headed to the kitchen for a drink. He watched her leave and ran a hand down his face when she was out of sight.

"He's got it bad." Kane told C.J. in certain terms. "I've never seen him look at anyone like he does her."

"I see what you mean. Unfortunately, I have to put a wrench in all the happiness. My interrogation shed some new light as to why Sam was being watched." At C.J. statement Robert joined them at the table, as if a mask were pulled over his face the old Robert was back. His eyes had turned cold and his face was a stoned mask.

"How will this new information affect my getting to the Chancellor?"

"Chancellor Lansing is expecting Matthew to deliver the disk personally," C.J. said. He watched Robert think over the implications and continued. He said his next words cautiously. "Sam will change into Matthew and take you to the Chancellor. You won't have to break into the mansion." C.J. knew he would have to have a better argument where Sam was concerned. He felt the rage building in Robert and Kane was close behind.

Sam reentered the room, was aware of the tension, and almost retreated. She put on a brave smile and strolled in, placed a cup of coffee in front of Robert, and took the seat next to him. She reached under the table, took his hand, and gave a gentle squeeze. He returned the gesture relaxed a little but his expression remained hard. "Why do these two look like they want to rip your throat out, C.J.?"

"I just told them you would be able to help get Robert into the mansion. As you can see they aren't happy with the idea."

"That's right. C.J. We can't let her go into a den of vipers. We promised to keep her safe," Kane shouted. "Man, if her father were here, we wouldn't be having this discussion." Kane put his head in his hands and groaned.

"I won't let her go in. I'll figure out another way in without using Sam." Robert grabbed Sam's hand tighter in a death grip. He dragged her into this and he'd do everything to keep her out of the bigger mess.

"We all promised to keep her safe. I see no other way to complete this mission. While you were gone I took a look at the mansion plans and security detail. You'd have to blow a hole in the wall just to get in that fortress." C.J. could hear the thoughts around the table and waited for a reply. Both men were trying to run a dozen different scenarios through without Sam and they all ended the same—failure.

"Are you sure there's no other way?" Sam broke the silence with her question.

"C.J. is right. I poured over the details again and again. I thought if I took a break an idea would come to me." Robert shook his head in frustration and got up to pace. "That is one secure mansion. The security detail alone is a small army," He glanced at Sam,. "I hate having to involve you. I didn't want to involve you or any citizens for that matter."

"I want to help. Pretoria needs me and I'm going to do it. Chancellor Lansing has to be stopped at all cost. My father once told me a time would come and our world would change. He has been preparing me for this since I was little and the others, too. For some reason the four of us, Nick, Niles, Jamie, and I were born the same day and have remained friends, each presenting a unique talent. If you don't let me, God help me, I will do it on my own."

Three men stared at her with their mouths hanging open in astonishment and couldn't believe what Sam said. "If that doesn't beat all." Kane gasped and stuttered out the words. Kane knew she had a determined streak but this was something new. To place herself and her friends in the direct line of fire, not knowing the out come could be deadly.

Robert was at a loss for words. He just glared at Sam not breaking eye contact. She refused to look away first. Her eyes expressed so much determination and love for her home planet. He knew he was beaten and any argument he made would be futile. "I see there is no other way to do this," he pointed at her, "but just remember I'm in charge. You do as I say when I say it and don't deviate from the plan." A huge smile broke across her face signaling her success. Robert thought her father was going to kill him when he found out she was going in to the vipers' den.

"What do we need to do first?" Kane asked as he grabbed for the compact computer to make a list.

"Did Nick give you access to their security system?" Sam remembered her father said. *Security can get sloppy, and if they don't rotate, they lose interest quickly. Always wait until the end of a shift to make your move.*

"Yes, why?" What was going on in that mind of hers? She had a sparkle in her eyes that could only mean trouble.

"Can I take a look? There maybe something you missed," Sam pulled his computer closer and found the program Nick sent. She studied the guards' patterns for a while. She was watching the back wall when she saw it. Quickly tapping keys she brought up another window placing a corner of the wall in full view. "I have it!" She exclaimed with an air of superiority.

"Have what?" Robert and Kane had been making a list of supplies and still discussing the injustice of having to involve her.

"A way in! Here, take a look," She turned the computer in their direction. "Watch the guards. See they don't go all the way over. It's nearing the end of their shift."

"Where is this exactly?" Kane inquired pulling up another map of the estate. Sam scanned the map and pointed at the far back corner.

"I never thought to watch the monitors," Robert mumbled. "Okay, we now have a way for Kane to get in unnoticed." He was going to have a long talk with Aron when he got back. It was humiliating to have a woman know more then him after eight years of active service and six of academy training. He felt like a fool missing a detail that was obvious to anyone.

"What's your plan to get off this transport with little fuss?" Kane inquired. He was already plotting how to get over that ten-foot wall as quickly as possible.

"We know Chancellor Lansing has been watching Sam. It's a good bet she knows where we are headed. She'll be waiting to see me taken into custody along with Sam. Mr. Matthew and Ms. Johnson will have to be taken off the transport after Sam and I have left. I don't want to take any chances she has someone watching. C.J., did I hear you say Sam will be meeting a diplomat with her papers?"

"Her father has made arrangements. Is that important?" he asked, clearly concerned.

"Yes, this diplomat is not going to be expecting her to be under arrest. We have to have our story straight, C.J. We need at least three military officers we can trust to escort us to a secure location. Can you arrange that?"

"Whatever you need, I can arrange before we reach Plutonus. You might as well stay at my home. It's secure and at the main military installation. How much more secure do you want?" C.J. gave a rare smile at Sam. He felt she would feel more comfortable there then anywhere else. Sam gave him a grateful smile at his offer.

"Kane, you will be one of our escorts, get a uniform. C.J., your house will do fine but we will be going to M.I. first. Only to make it look good, we'll use the time to make contact with our commanders and gather our supplies. I'll talk to the commanding officer on board concerning our two prisoners," Robert looked at his watch. "We should be landing in about two hours. Everyone be ready. Sam try and get some rest."

Robert and Kane left the room to coordinate with military security and C.J. made a few phone calls. "Sam. Here's a picture of Mr. Matthew; take the time to practice his shape and form." Sam nodded and sat on the bed practicing till she became tired again.

CHAPTER 21

SAM COULDN'T sleep and eagerly awaited her first view of Plutonus from a private observation deck. As the planet came into view she saw a marble of orange and yellow colors swirling around the planet. She had read the planet was in decay, but seeing it with her own eyes told a different story.

A hundred years ago before there was a colony on Pretoria everyone lived on Plutonus. It was wired, wild, and full of bustling factories. After many decades of waste and pollution, the citizens were forced into climate-controlled domes. Temperatures soared to 120 degrees, and the land became barren. The problem reached critical conditions when vegetation and crops began to die from the toxic air. The government organized an expedition to explore other worlds and find a vegetation rich planet.

When the reports came back that Pretoria was the perfect planet to use for food growth, the leaders of Plutonus colonized Pretoria. They turned it into a farming and education colony. Learning from their past mistakes, the laws on Pretoria were strict. No one but government officials had cars and they only could use clean burning fuel. Everything on Pretoria ran on solar power to keep the air clean. Most citizens lived in domes and transportation was limited to mass transit pods. There were fields of flowing golden grain as far as the eye could see. Orchards spanned the area in their colorful glory. Flowers and plants grew plentiful and the water ran clear and pure.

Sam was joined by Robert and another officer who hung back by the door, giving them some privacy. "The planet looks so peaceful and clean from up here. It's hard to believe the atmosphere is toxic." Sam stared out the window as they came closer to the surface. The peaceful view turned into rusted metal structures and deserts thousands of miles wide. In the distance there was a raging dust storm making visibility minimal. Sam had turned away from the window. She couldn't believe the destruction. How could someone destroy something that was once so beautiful? The fact that her government had made such a terrible mistake broke her heart.

Robert gathered her close and walked her back to the room. He never would have brought her if he knew the sight was going to do this to her. The view always gave him pause, a reminder of the beauty that once was and could be again. The beauty by his side would have to be enough for now.

Kane answered the door to their room a short time later and three military officers entered. "Are we ready, sir?" Kane looked over to Robert and he nodded.

Robert walked over to Sam with an officer close behind. "It's time to go. The cuffs will be loose enough, so they won't hurt." The officer handed Robert the cuffs and he placed them on her. He turned around and Kane secured his cuffs. They formed a procession Sam flanked by Kane and one officer. Robert followed with CJ and the other officers. The exiting passengers made room for the procession working its way toward the main concourse. At the exit was a diplomat surrounded by more officers, the expression on his face was one of confusion.

"What seems to be going on here?" The diplomat sent by her father asked the officer in charge.

"I was informed they were prisoners of Barnabas Matthew and they were to be escorted to Military Intel for interrogation."

"There must be some mistake," the diplomat stammered. "I was supposed to deliver her credentials. Then I was to take her to a safe location." He became nervous when he realized the officer wasn't going to release Sam into his custody. The diplomat clutched the papers he was holding tighter.

The officer held out his hand for the papers. "I'll take them and see that she receives them when we're done." The diplomat reluctantly handed over the papers.

"Miss Gabriels, if you need my assistance don't hesitate to contact me. My number is on the card enclosed with your papers. I'll contact your father to advise him of your arrival and situation." The diplomat was visibly sweating and looked ready to faint. He glanced between Sam and Robert still in confusion.

"Thank you. When you speak to him, tell him don't forget to feed Niles." She smiled at the diplomat to put him at ease.

"I'll be sure to give him the message." They stepped out into the gray night where a vehicle was waiting to transport them to the military installation.

"How are you holding up?" Robert asked Sam, looking down at her slim bound wrist.

"I'm okay. I thought that diplomat was going to cause a scene." She could tell from the tone in his voice that he thought this was her first time in cuffs. He would be shocked with what her father had taught them. She carried a small weapon that didn't look like anything but a harmless hairpin.

"I did, too. He looked like he was ready to jump out of his skin. I almost felt sorry for him," he chuckled.

"You almost felt sorry for him. I did, the poor man. I can imagine his conversation with my father." Her father would play it up and that poor man would be bowing at his feet. He'd eventually call him back when everything was clear and the mission completed.

"He'll be okay once your father starts laughing about Niles. Is that supposed to be a code word?" Kane inquired in obvious delight of the diplomat's nervousness.

"That's another thing my father and I arranged. When I was little we would use Niles if I was safe and Nick if I was in danger." The information had been drilled into her head from at a young age. Each of them had their own code phrase or word. They had other codes for locations and destinations. The four of them used them often for meeting times and places.

Kane laughed. "Nick was always more trouble than Niles. Do you need me to loosen the cuffs?" He saw her wince when she turned to look behind her.

"They're pinching, but they're okay. We're almost there right?"

"A little further, miss," the driver said in reply.

"When we arrive there will be more officers, but they're just for show. We wanted to make this look believable to anyone watching," C.J. said.

The sky was turning a light gray when they arrived at the installation. The compound was heavily guarded. Sam saw watch towers every fifty feet and a huge wall extending far to the right and left. C.J. saw that Sam was taking in her surroundings. "It's not as bad as it looks. Wait till we get inside. Pretoria looks better, but this will do." Sam didn't respond, she was looking at the layout and security detail trying to memorize what she saw. It was one of the first rules her father taught her—beware of your surroundings. Find all possible exits and weapons. C.J. was right, the inside was a little better. It looked like a small community with shops and offices. They stopped in front of a white building and armed officers streamed out to form two lines leading from the door to the vehicle.

"Do you think they over did it?" Kane commented. He exited the vehicle and opened the door to take Sam by the arm. "Don't forget to struggle." He moved her quickly inside and to the interrogation room they were assigned. Kane stayed with Sam, while Robert, under protest, was escorted down the hall struggling.

Sam looked unsure and asked, "Kane what's going on? Why did they take Robert to a different room?"

"This maneuver was just protocol, sit back and calm down," he answered, keeping a close watch on the door. He was trying to show he wasn't worried about the separation, they had agreed they needed to stick together. Robert was going to be pissed.

Some time later, in walked a sizeable older man with short graying dark hair and horn-rimmed glasses. He was dressed elegantly in a tux as if he were on his way to the theater. He casually took a seat across from Sam and crossed his arms on the table. He peered intently at her for a moment then spoke. "Detective Michaels, please introduce this young lady to me and explain why she is still in cuffs. I understand we have her to thank for Barnabas Matthew and Francis Johnson."

Kane hurried over to remove the handcuffs from Sam and make introductions. He was stunned at the General's appearance, here of all places. Why was he here? "Sam Gabriels, this is the Chancellor of Military Intel, General Ronin. General Ronin this is Sam Gabriels."

"It's a pleasure to meet you, sir." Sam wasn't sure whether she should stand up and salute or pass out. It was an honor to meet a Chancellor—only a few had ever met them personally.

"The pleasure is always mine," A huge grin broke across his face. "How is your father doing? I understand he had something to do with your being here."

"My father was safe when I left. He's only part of the reason I'm here. This became personal when the cell had me tailed. My father meant no harm when he started the alliance. He only wished to help the citizens of Pretoria."

"Settle down, I agree with your father. It's time for some changes. Colonel Michaels and C.J. have updated me and I realize you're the only way he will be able to finish his mission. They said you're very special and bring a unique talent to the group. I also understand your friends have been valuable assets in discovering vital cell members and hard evidence to convict them."

"They have, sir," Kane replied. "Without their assistance things could have escalated beyond Pretoria's boundaries."

"My friends and I are all unique. We've formed our own information and supply network." Sam felt she had to defend her friends before opinions could be formulated. His next comment relaxed her considerably.

"Your leadership skills are commendable. You're so much like your father. I've seen battles lost because of weak leadership."

"Thank you. I had a good teacher," she blushed.

"Now, I think I've left the Colonel and C.J. waiting long enough.

I expected him to break down the door by now. He was upset when we separated the two of you. I thought it would be best if my officers saw you independently interrogated. I've never seen him act like this." Kane was trying to hold back a chuckle. The Chancellor opened the door and asked the officer to bring them to this room. They heard shouting in the hall and the door burst open. There stood Robert and C.J. They stopped when they saw the Chancellor sitting with Sam. Robert was the first to move, he immediately stood behind Sam placing a hand on her shoulder followed by C.J. He winked down at Sam in a show of support.

"Sir, is there a problem?" C.J. asking with an imposing tone in his voice.

Chancellor Ronin took in the impressive sight. Never before had he seen such unity and they'd only known her a short time. "No, Colonel, Miss Gabriels and I were having a nice chat. Her father and I go way back. C.J., I understand they will be staying with you until mission completion."

"Yes, sir, they will. I felt Sam would feel more secure and comfortable."

"Good," He'd never seen his interrogator act this way either. He sized up his Colonel next. "When can I expect that to be, Colonel?"

"We're still working out a few details and will need back up." He looked at his commander for reinforcement.

"I can give you back up only when the mission is completed. I don't want too many knowing what's going on yet." He had a look a resigned sympathy when he made the statement.

"I figured that, sir. I had to ask. We'll need weapons and explosives. Ours were confiscated when we boarded the transport carrier." He handed the General the list they'd made.

"I'll have it done within the hour. Do you need a layout of the mansion?"

"No, I already have that. The only way in is through the front door without using explosives." The chancellor was stunned at the announcement and took a minute to think before he spoke again.

"How did you get plans already?" Sam began to squirm in her chair.

Robert and Kane looked at each other and nodded. "We have a certain computer genius on Pretoria that was able to help."

"I see, and you're not going to tell me anymore, are you?" The Chancellor kept his hands folded on the table and appraised the three men and one woman. The three men behind Sam all smiled at the Chancellor. He stood up and prepared to leave. "Very well. Colonel, I will see you back here at eight hundred hours with mission completed. Understood?"

"I understand, sir. May I have a private word with you?" Chancellor Ronin nodded and headed toward the door.

"What is it, Colonel?" He walked a ways down the hall then stopped and turned toward his Colonel. He looked troubled and unsure of himself, which was unusual. Robert was always in control.

"I need your assurance that Sam—Miss Gabriels will be safe. If anything were to happen to Kane or me, she needs to be sent back to Pretoria no matter how this goes down."

So she is Sam to him, the Chancellor thought *It seems that enchantress in there had broken through his soldiers' hard shell.* He placed an encouraging hand on Robert's shoulder. "You have my word. She'll be on the next carrier out after your mission. She will only be released into her father's custody. Even if I have to escort her myself, she will be protected."

"Thank you, sir." The Chancellor left Robert slumped against the wall to collect his thoughts. The door to interrogation opened and Kane walked out first. He straightened up quickly before Sam could see him.

"Is everything good to go?" Kane asked, eyeing his cousin with worry.

"Yes. Let's get out of here." C.J. exited the room with Sam and he had a hand on her elbow to lend support. She had put up a brave front for the Chancellor, and now was showing her fatigue.

"I'll show you to my place and then I have to return for Mr. Matthew and Ms. Johnson," They left by a series of tunnels that lead to an electronics shop. A vehicle was waiting for them, a few blocks more was a two-story townhouse that belonged to C.J.. They pulled into the garage and entered through the kitchen. "Sam, if you'll follow me, I'll show you to your room." Their bags had been delivered while they were at Military Intel and were waiting inside the door.

Sam was very tired and looked forward to a restful sleep. Before she left Pretoria, Jamie had given her a pinch of pink powder. She told her it would help her sleep, but only for a couple of hours. She was going to need the sleep to clear her mind for the task ahead. She followed C.J. to a modest sized, simply decorated room with a double bed and a private bath. "I think you'll be comfortable here. There are towels in the bathroom closet."

"Thanks, C.J. I'll be down in a little while. I need some tea to help me sleep." She placed her bag at the end of the bed and gathered the things she would need.

"I'll have it waiting for you." He backed out trying to avoid the emotions coming off her. She was one person who doesn't block her emotions. He felt her uncertainty of the future, her fear for her family and friends, and the exhaustion of her mind.

Sam took a long hot bath and changed into one of the new pajama outfits she bought. Robert was the only one in the kitchen and he turned at the sound of soft footsteps. There on the bottom step as if rooted there, was Sam in a pair of dark blue silk pajamas, her long red hair streaming down her back in soft waves. She froze and looked at him. He had shaved and his blond hair glistened with dampness. He was dressed only in a pair of camouflage pants and holding a rather large sandwich that was starting to drip sauce on the floor. "You might want to put that on a plate," she said, pointing to the sandwich.

He quickly looked down and grabbed a plate. He cleaned up the mess and cut the sandwich in half. "Would you like half?" She moved to the stove and poured the tea C.J. had made for her.

"No, thank you. Just tea. I'm going to take it up with me and get some sleep." She retreated upstairs, leaving him watching after her. Kane came down and snapped his fingers to attain his attention. He laughed when Robert blinked and tried to hit him. He dodged the blow and moved over to the fridge.

"What are your intentions when this is over?" He grabbed a drink from the fridge and took a seat, turned the chair around, and straddled it. He had propped his hands over the back and was measuring his cousin's reaction.

Robert took his plate and joined him. He scowled at his cousin's question. "Who are you, her father?"

"No, a concerned friend of both parties involved. I look out for her when her father can't. Aron calls me before he leaves town. I've been keeping an eye on her for a while now."

His first meeting with Aron felt like an interview. He had attended a gathering at the chief's home celebrating his fathers seventy-fifth birthday. After a strange meeting with grandpa McGovens, Aron showed up asking all kinds of questions. Where he went to school, where he did his training, how long had he served and the last question was really weird. Aron asked what he thought about the girls. He hit Kane on the back and told him he would do. A week later, Aron called to tell Kane he'd be out of town and asked if he'd keep an eye on them. Kane didn't dare refuse.

"Hell if I know," Robert said, running a hand through his still damp hair in frustration. "First, I have to live through this mission and protect her. What do you mean you've been watching her?"

"You're the best and with my help, we're unstoppable." Kane refused to answer his last question for fear it would start an argument or worse. He opened his drink and took a long swallow.

Robert eyed his cousin curiously. "How can you be so confident?" He knew his cousin was avoiding his question and decided a discussion would wait till later.

I've seen you in action. Robert, you always complete your mission even if your injured," Kane pointed out; the man at times seemed indestructible.

Robert grinned and said, "I remember." He had been shot in the leg, left shoulder and his right eye had been damaged on their last mission. His target was in sight and he struggled the last yard under heavy gunfire when the target was eliminated Robert passed out. He awoke in the military hospital with his artificial eye and multiple stitches. That mission gave Robert his current rank and a medal for bravery under fire.

Lying on the table between them was the infamous disk. Kane tapped it and said, "Have you seen all the information on this?"

"No, I haven't, but I can just imagine what it contains." Robert wasn't sure he wanted to know what was on the disk. There could be information that could incriminate other high-ranking officials including his superior.

"Why don't we load it up and see what's on it? C.J. left your compact." Kane reached behind him and placed it on the table in front of him.

When he wasn't looking, Kane stole half of the sandwich and Robert growled. "Go make your own."

Kane snatched it back and said, "But yours taste so much better." Robert turned on his compact and a message came up from Nick.

CHAPTER 22

ROBERT — *Go ahead and read the disk, but stay away from the files marked Hilary. When Chancellor Lansing enters her password an e-mail virus will start causing her system to lock up. Do not use the password "PHOBIA." I wouldn't want to buy you a new computer. If something happens and you need time, run the program called Lone Wolf. It will shut down all video communication on Plutonus temporarily. The program will buy you twenty minutes to regroup. Keep Sam safe, we'll be awaiting your call.*
– Nick.

"I don't believe this; he thought of everything. Look at this, Kane," Robert turned the computer in Kane's direction.

"Nick was always messing with computers at the station. We had a virus once that started eating away at the hard drive, and the chief called Nick. He had our computers up and running in no time. He was even able to recover the corrupted data. I wouldn't want to be his enemy."

"That's what I'm afraid of if we don't bring Sam back unharmed. We're going to have to move to a different planet." The mood turned somber as Robert tapped the keyboard, revealing the decoded information. The disk included a list of past targets, operatives who worked for the cell, supply schedules, and a partial list of gifted citizens. The files included names, addresses, and their gifts. Sam's name was at the top linked with Mattie's. There were several other names as suspected gifted. Robert opened another file with Francis Johnson's name. There were memos concerning past missions and possible future targets. One target made Robert's heart stop. Plans had been made to blow up the training center a week from today. "It looks like I'll be returning to Pretoria with you, Kane." He turned the computer again so he could see the information.

"Shit. That explains whey they were gathering in Luella. What time do we begin?"

"We leave here at eighteen hundred hours and head back to M.I. have Sam change into Matthew there. You follow and station yourself outside this area," he said, pointing to the library wall on the layout. "Her office is located here on an upper level. Niles seems to think there's a lot of equipment up here. From the diagram, there are at least a hundred outlets."

There was a knock at the kitchen and door both men took precautions. Kane moved out of sight while Robert approached the door. "Colonel Michaels? C.J. sent me with the items you requested. He also said don't forget to feed Niles," Both men laughed and opened the door. A timid looking officer stood on the other side and visible swallowed at the sight of Kane and Robert. They both still had their weapons out and were without shirts showing their toned muscles and numerous scars. "Here are the things you requested, Colonel."

"Good," Robert closed the door in the officer's face and carried the bags to the table. He started pulling out electronic devices; one was a set of micro communication transmitters. "We'll keep in touch with these. When Sam and I pull up to the gate, you get into position and use our old call signal." He pulled another item out that looked like handcuffs.

"Very nice. Breakable handcuffs." Kane picked up and admired the piece.

"I have to be able to break free at the perfect moment." The next item was a package about the size of a small brick and gray in color.

Kane's smile grew enormous. "You didn't forget. You remembered. How kind," The last few items were a small arsenal of weapons—night scopes and contoured body armor—one for each of them. "Why did they send these?" Kane asked as he fingered the vest.

"I requested them. I'm not taking any chances with Sam by our side. Now, back to work. We'll enter through the front, and you will be stationed here," Robert pointed to a position on the map again. "Wait for us to hand over the disk and get into her office. Once Nick's program begins to run Chancellor Lansing will panic. Wait for my signal before blowing the wall open. It may be our only exit if things go wrong."

They took a few more minutes to go over the plan. Kane gave a call to Chief McGovens with a situation update and to be on the look out for suspicious activity on the training center campus. Robert took a minute to call his commander and e-mailed a copy of the memos to Chancellor Ronin.

"Sam, wake up," Robert said in hushed tones. He had been trying to wake Sam for the last fifteen minutes. He resorted to another tactic. He bent down and started to whisper in her ear everything he would like to do to her if only she would wake up. He got the desired response he wanted when Sam reached her arms around his neck and blinked her eyes open. "Good evening, Sam," he said in a husky voice. "Were you having a nice dream?"

She smiled beautifully up at him. "Was it only a dream? I thought I was in heaven," He gave her a gentle kiss. She tasted so sweet that it was hard to stop. With a sigh of regret he lowered her arms from around his neck.

"Unfortunately, we don't have more time. We need to leave soon." She stretched and sat up in bed, noticing the body armor.

"What's this for?" she asked, eyeballing it inquisitively.

"It's for your protection. There might be a time when I can't protect you. Will you wear it, please?" Sam kept peeking at the vest, and with a resigned sigh she picked it up to check its weight.

She gazed into his eyes; what she saw the made her heart jump. There was a flash of concern then steel that she wasn't about to argue with. She quickly agreed. "I'll wear it."

"Meet me downstairs in fifteen minutes with this on," he pointed to the armor she now held.

Kane appeared at the bottom of the steps dressed all in black. "Is she ready?"

"Almost, I found this on the nightstand. It took me awhile to wake her up." He was holding up a bag with pink powder residue in it.

Kane took the packet from him to inspect it. "Jamie gave her a sleeping packet."

Robert became enraged at the thought. "What possessed her to take it now?"

Kane backed up and allowed him to pass. Robert started pacing the kitchen. As his anger grew his pace quickened. He'd seen that face before and the person on the receiving end never boded well. Hardened soldiers had wept after a lashing from their Colonel. Sam would need help calming his temper if she came down too soon. A little interference now might go a long way to cushion the final blow.

"She needed the rest. Give her a little credit. Jamie didn't give her that much, only enough for a few hours of undisturbed sleep."

"Jamie will have to answer a few questions when we get back. I don't like her taking anything before a mission," Robert shouted.

Kane was quick to defend her actions. He knew of one quick way to grab his cousin's attention and his words would have to count. "Jamie would never put her in jeopardy. Give it a rest. She's not one of your soldiers."

Silently observing the exchange from the shadowed stairway was the object of their discussion. When she heard Kane and Robert arguing she waited a moment and listened. Thoughts ran through her mind of the things he had spoken. Her little secret was that she heard everything he had whispered to her. It was hard to restrain her feelings, a real test of will not to react. She wanted to pull him down beside her and have him do all those things he promised. She longed to show him her true feelings, but the time wasn't right. She wasn't sure a time would ever come. The world was changing fast and there may not be a tomorrow for them. She wiped away a stray tear, took a deep breath, and moved out of the shadows. "I'm ready. When do we leave?"

Both men were startled at her appearance in the kitchen. Kane recovered first. "We leave shortly. Have a seat and I'll go over the mission with you."

Robert had turned away and made busy at the counter. He was

trying to get his emotions in check. If he were to look at her now she would see how much he cared for her—maybe she'd think he loved her. Love? Could it be? He shook his head to get the thought out and decided to examine it later, after this mess was over. He had to put his mind completely on the mission, heart and mind of ice, no room for warmth. This was another mission that had to be completed; failure was not an option.

He was still standing at the counter when C.J. returned. He took in the kitchen scene and didn't miss a thing. He sensed the electric current between the three, a strange mixture emotional tension he couldn't move, his mind wouldn't let him pass. C.J. had to break the tension. "Are you ready?" Three pairs of eyes focused on him and some of the tension dissolved into thin air.

"We're ready," Robert said with ice in his voice.

"Niles, do you recall those stories grandpa McGovens used to tell us?" Jamie was sitting in the window seat again watching the street below. He came over and sat opposite her, bending a knee and placing his arm across it.

"You know I do. Why?" Jamie had been quiet most of the night. She'd wander aimlessly about the apartment like a caged animal. Annie tried to encourage her to rest and Jamie just kept moving. She'd finally settled as darkness fell.

"Could you tell me one?" she asked quietly, wiping away a tear.

"Which one would you like to hear?" Niles reached out and toyed with a strand of silky blond hair.

"Wasn't there a story about an enchantress?" Her gaze connected with his and he recollected the story just like grandpa told it. Niles sucked in a breath and held it in for a minute.

"Yes," He smiled, remembering clearly. "It was called the soldier and the enchantress."

"Could you tell it like your grandpa would? All I need is one of the barn kittens," Jamie's smile reached all the way to her eyes. She had many fond memories of the farm outside Luella, so many adventures.

"Gather around my children and listen well, for I have a story to tell." His voice came out silky and deep. Nick came over and took a seat on the floor. He could almost smell the hay and horses when Niles spoke that way.

"This is the story of the soldier and the enchantress. Her path had been set from birth, and she was destined for greatness it was told. Her father trained her and her friends day after day with the skill of a warrior. He told them a time will come and our world will change and only then would they realize their greatest powers.

"What he didn't tell his daughter was that she could change her appearance just with a thought. Her mother protected her with charms, hiding her gift until the time was right. Time passed, and she grew into a beautiful woman with hair of fire and eyes of emeralds. She was admired by many soldiers, but only one caught her attention. A great tragedy occurred one day. Her mother and father had been taken by an evil witch and hidden away. The evil witch wanted the enchantress' gift in order to enslave the worlds. The enchantress and her friends sought out the soldier for help.

"Little did the enchantress know, the soldier had been watching her and knew of her struggles. He had fallen in love with her at first sight and would do anything for her. She only had to ask. He rescued her parents with the help of his and her friends. Her gift became known and she feared for her life. The soldier promised to protect her. A great battle ensued and the witch was tricked. Together they saved the worlds from the evil witch's rule. The governing powers praised them for their efforts and rewarded them with rank and title.

"The soldier waited to confess his love until all was safe. He took her to a garden of roses and presented her with a ring as unique as she. From their love grew others, but alas my children, that is another story."

"Do you think it's true, Niles?" Jamie asked with stars in her eyes.

"Maybe. Grandpa was never very specific when I asked. He always said time will tell."

"The similarities are eerie," Nick shivered.

"I believe your grandfathers' stories. It's why you were all trained together. I went to him the day Sam showed Jamie the gym. He told me it wasn't a coincidence that you were all born the same day. I can't remember his exact words, but he did say, 'teach them well.'" Aron came over and laid a hand on Niles' shoulder.

"Did he ever tell you his stories, Mr. Gabriels?" Jamie questioned.

"No, he said they were for your ears only. Today is the first I have ever heard one of them." Aron took in the three friends now grown and longed for his daughter's safe return.

CHAPTER 23

SAM COULDN'T believe the change in Robert. He had been so tender earlier, and now his face was stone hard cold. Even his voice sent shivers down her spine, and not the shivers of delight she would prefer when he spoke. Kane had been rather silent also as if they were preparing for the worst. She closed her eyes, practiced her breathing exercises and tried to remain calm. They arrived at the electronics shop and entered the tunnels. No one spoke when they entered Military Intel's office. It had been cleared of all non-essential personnel, and only a select few remained. Robert was handcuffed and Sam turned into Barnabas Matthew as they left the building. Kane left in a separate vehicle with C.J.

Robert didn't speak again until they were almost to Chancellor Lansings'. "Kane, do you copy?"

"I copy, Robert."

"Take your position. We're almost at the gate."

"Will do."

They approached the front gates and were greeted by armed security. "Present your identification and state your business."

Sam handed over Barnabas papers and Roberts. "I'm here to deliver this prisoner and a diplomatic pouch to Chancellor Lansing. She is expecting me."

The security officer handed the papers back and opened the

gate. His partner called up to the house and waved them through. They proceeded forward along a long winding drive lined with security lights and stopped before the front doors. "Don't forget make it look convincing." Robert looked at Sam and smiled. The Robert she knew was back, if only temporarily.

They exited the vehicle and heard an owls hoot and knew Kane was nearby waiting for the signal. The door opened and they were greeted by another officer. "This way please. The Chancellor has been waiting."

Robert was scanning the area and counting the number of guards and exits. Sam gave him a little push to start him walking and in a gruff voice told him to move. The library doors opened and there stood a smiling Chancellor Lansing. The library was very large with no windows and shelves lined with a multitude of books reached the ceiling. To the left there was a set of stairs leading to a glass enclosed office with over a hundred monitors and one overly large television.

"Ah, Mr. Matthew. What took so long? I was expecting you yesterday. I see you brought the traitor with you. Why wasn't he eliminated on Pretoria?"

"We ran into a few problems and had to tie up some loose ends. I have the disk," Sam produced the disk and approached Chancellor Lansing. "I've already checked it out. I brought you the traitor. I thought you might like to eliminate him yourself." She took the disk and proceeded up to her office.

"Bring him with us while I personally check this out. Then you can eliminate him like you were supposed to." They followed her up the stairs. In the office the monitors were blinking and each one was labeled with an address.

She recognized one address in particular because it was her home on Pretoria. From the angle of the house it looked to be on the light pole outside her home. Sam felt sick to her stomach, but remained calm. She sensed Robert stiffen behind her. "Is this how you kept tabs on us?" she asked, motioning to the monitors.

Hilary looked up from her desk and answered. "Of course. How else could I know you were doing your job right?" Hilary inserted the disk, began to load the program, and entered her password—"Phobia."

Distracting her, Sam asked another question. "Are you planning to tell me why you had me following Sam Gabriels?"

With a smug look on her face, the Chancellor explained. "She's a pet project of mine; she's not only the alliance leader's daughter, but also a mimic. A while back, my cousin called to say the neighbor girl had changed into the postman. She'll be the first of my slaves. Once I control her, I can control Pretoria and Plutonus. She will be a nice addition to my staff." She glanced down and panic seized her when she saw the data going to the other Chancellors, Military Intel, CERT, and every computer on both Pretoria and Plutonus.

She rapidly pushed the panic button under her desk alerting security, and frantically tried to stop the program, but her keyboard had locked up. When the virus had run its course, every monitor had the same message blinking "TIME'S UP!"

She rounded the desk in a rage and stalked towards Sam. "You idiot! You've ruined every plan I've put in motion, everything I have worked for the last five years!" She raised her hands to strangle Sam. She changed into Hilary in defensive mode. Hilary stopped dead in her tracks and blinked rapidly. She couldn't believe her eyes. She put a hand to her chest and gasped for breath.

"I'm here to tell you that I know your plan and it's not going to work." At that moment there was an explosion causing paper and bright orange flames to fly about the library. Sam took advantage of Lansing's distraction and cold cocked her, sending her to the floor. Robert broke his bonds and Kane entered the library through a gaping hole in the wall.

"Am I too late?" he called up, grinning at Robert.

Chancellor Lansing had regained her senses and attacked Sam. She was trying to remove Hilary's hands from her neck when security broke down the door. With a flood of bullets they entered and took positions around the room. Hilary tried to use Sam's stunned state to escape by pushing past her, but Sam was quicker. She swept her foot and tripped her. Robert quickly moved to the bottom of the stairs where Kane was waiting with a weapons cache. Sam grabbed a hold of Hilary's hair to tug backward, but she managed to flip Sam. They ended up tumbling down the stairs right into the line of fire. Hilary crawled out of reach and moved away toward the door with Sam in pursuit.

Robert took aim at Chancellor Lansing, but was confused as to which one was Sam. Remembering what her father said he yelled out, "Samantha, get down and out of the way!"

Sam changed back and hit the floor moving out of the line of sight. She watched as gunfire erupted and Robert trained his weapon on Chancellor Hilary Lansing. Time seemed to slow down as the bullet entered the chamber, the trigger was pulled, and the report was heard. Chancellor Lansing slowly descended to the floor and fell into a crumpled heap. The firing stopped when an officer yelled, "Cease fire!"

Robert and Kane were now standing in the middle of the room back to back, surveying the damage. In the distance the sound of sirens signaled Military Intel's arrival. They were franticly searching through the bodies of injured and dead looking for Sam. "Where is she?" Robert moved his way back over to the stairs and yelled above all the chaos, "Samantha, where are you?"

He finally found her safe, curled in a ball, eyes closed under Chancellor Lansing's desk. She was repeating the phrase "this is the time of change." There were tears streaking down her face, and he tried to pull her out but she fought back. She recognized the voice calling to her. It was Robert. Her heart began to beat faster. She gave up her fight and allowed him to gently pull her out from under the desk. He gathered her into his arms and whispered, "Sam, it's over. Open you eyes and look at me."

"I thought you would die down there," She pounded on his chest and he gathered her closer burying her face under his chin.

He murmured in her ear, "I'm here now and I'm not letting go." He picked her up and with Kane leading the way, he carried her down to the waiting vehicle. C.J. opened the door and he climbed in holding her on his lap all the way back to the military installation. She heard C.J., Kane, and Robert talking in low voices.

"Is she going to be all right?" Kane asked.

Robert with his cheek resting in Sam's hair answered, "It will take some time just like it did for us."

Sam woke up disoriented when she realized she wasn't at home. The memories came rushing back and she began to cry again. A warm arm pulled her close and whispered, "Go ahead and cry, I'm here with you. It's safe to sleep." Robert gently kissed her and she fell back asleep.

It was morning before she woke again, alone this time. She sat up and rubbed the sleep from her eyes. *Was she dreaming?* She wondered. She moved to the window and saw the dark clouds of pollution and toxic air. A shiver ran through her body and she didn't notice that she was being watched.

Robert was standing in the doorway watching the angel before him dressed in a white t-shirt. He crawled into bed with her last night when he heard her cry out. C.J. told him to go to her; she needed his strength. He had to speak soft words to her before she would relax and sleep peacefully. It was a real test of willpower on his part when she willingly kissed him back. She tasted so sweet and her skin was as soft as a rose petal.

She turned around and eyed Robert's grinning face. He was standing there with no shirt, jeans unbuttoned and his hair was disheveled. She took a tentative step toward him. "What are you grinning at?"

"Did I ever tell you that you look lovely in the morning?" He swallowed a sip of his coffee to hide his smirk.

"No. This is the first time," she answered.

"Well, you do. Do you feel up to traveling?" Robert asked with concern. She had a few bruises where Hilary had grabbed her throat. On her legs were more bruises. The emotional scars would be the worst. *She may never recover from them,* he thought

Sam looked down at her clasped hands and quietly she asked, "Did everything really happen last night? My memories are a little foggy this morning." He put his cup down, captured her hands, led her to a chair, and kneeled before her. He looked directly into her tear stained face and wished he could take away the pain. He'd give anything to put that sparkle back in her eyes.

He answered after a few moments of silence. "Yes, it all happened. You and your friends have opened the door. There is no stopping Pretoria from the path to freedom. It seems we have caused an uprising. There has been an unbelievable response from the citizens of both planets. The Chancellors have been forced to pass new legislation allowing for inventions to be completed on Pretoria and you, my dear, don't have to hide your gift anymore." He gave her time to absorb the implications of his declaration.

Realizing what he had said made the fear dissipate and as if great weight had been lifted from her shoulders, she beamed up at Robert. "I'm ready to go home now. When do we leave?"

The phone rang in the distance breaking the spell surrounding the couple. Robert rose and pulled Sam into an embrace crushing her body to his hard length. A cough sounded behind them, and Robert touched his forehead to hers. "Not now, Kane." Sam giggled and tried to back away, but he held fast and kept her by his side. He whispered in her ear, "You're not getting away that easy. We have unfinished business."

"Robert, this can't wait. Our presence is requested in the High Chancellors conference room. Our escort will be arriving shortly."

"I've already made my report to Chancellor Ronin. What could the others want?" Robert pulled her even closer, not wanting to let go.

"I'm just following orders," Kane looked at Sam with a note of sorrow. "You'll be joining us also."

"Why does she need to go?" Robert had stiffened beside her. She could feel his anger growing.

"They only said a car will be coming to pick all of us up," He held up his hands. "Don't shoot the messenger."

Sam moved away from Robert and prepared to get dressed. Robert stormed out of the room bellowing for C.J. He couldn't understand why they would need to see her. He had arisen early that morning, filed his report, and made arrangements for passage back to Pretoria. He wanted to get Sam as far away from this damn planet as fast possible.

She entered the living room wearing a dress of dark green with a matching scarf and her hair was pulled neatly back in a braid. C.J. stopped speaking to admire the vision. Robert noticed he had lost his attention and turned around. His breath caught in his throat and Kane took her hand. "You look lovely in that dress. I had my reservations when you picked it out, but now, it's perfect. This way your chariot waits," He led her to the front door and out onto the drive.

The other two men followed behind Robert was scowling at Kane's back all the way to the car. Waiting out front was a procession of vehicles and an armed escort. The three men had dressed in regulation uniform and were an impressive sight walking down the drive.

Robert being the highest ranked officer present entered the Chancellors chamber first, followed by C.J., then Kane escorting Sam. At the end of the table sat the three remaining Chancellors. Chancellor Ronin spoke first. "Here they are now," He walked over and pulled out a chair for Sam. "Please take a seat my dear." They complied and looked puzzled with the reception.

"It has been decided by this council that an interim Chancellor be selected immediately to replace Chancellor Lansing. By the laws of Plutonus and Pretoria the council of three can choose without election. We have chosen your father, Aron Gabriels, to fill the position based on his years of service and leadership skills. We believe him to be the only choice. Before you say anything, we are aware of his activities as the alliance leader. C.J., you will be his temporary advisor until such a time he deems your services no longer necessary. A diplomat has been dispatched along with proper security for your family, Miss Gabriels."

"It will be an honor to serve beside him, sir," C.J. said, stunned that he was being released from his current duties.

"You do understand that you'll be living on Pretoria?" The Chancellor asked, not sure of C.J.'s reaction to the news.

Then C.J. beamed and said, "That will be a nice change, thank you."

"Colonel Michaels and Detective Michaels, it has also come to our attention that there is still a potential threat on Pretoria. A possible plot has been discovered that puts the training center in Luella in danger. You two have been chosen to head a new division of M.I. that will monitor and disband any remaining cell members. The Provincial Police Chief will be coordinating with you when any manpower is needed. Detective Michaels, you will retain your rank of Major and all authority that goes with it."

"Thank you, sir. Where will we be based?" Kane asked with hesitation.

"Of course you would remain on Pretoria, bearing some travel. We need you right in the center of activity." Chancellor Ronin remarked and smiled. He focused his attention on Sam next.

"On a more serious note, Miss Gabriels, you have broken numerous laws including, but not limited to, invasion of privacy, illegal use of herbal medicines, false identity, and failure to alert the authorities of your friends' illegal activities."

Sam was speechless. She didn't know how to answer to the Chancellors' accusations. The three men stood up and were about to speak at once. "Wait, Chancellor—"

He held up a hand, stopping them. "Please hear me out first before going off in a rage. In light of recent circumstances, this council is willing to over look your crimes, only if you agree to head a group of scientists to set up a school for gifted citizens."

C.J. still stood behind Sam, his face turned red with rage. "You will not be setting this school up here on Plutonus. I will not stand by and watch innocent children be removed from their homes again. It was cruel when it was done to me. I have no memory of my parents or my home. This is an outrage! I will not put up with this injustice another moment. I promised her father she would be safe with me and she will be returning to Pretoria today."

"Please take your seat and let me finish. The school will be built on Pretoria and children will be able to come and go as they please. We have learned from our mistakes once again. The school will be a way for scientist to study the gifted and help students learn to refine and control their gifts. Apparently there is more to learn about Pretoria's environment than was first discovered." He focused his attention on Sam again. "This is an enormous undertaking, Miss Gabriels. Do you think you are up to the challenge?" The Chancellor looked up at C.J. and said, "Of course C.J. will assist you and I believe your friends also need an outlet for their talents."

C.J. had taken his seat next to Sam at the Chancellors announcement. She laid a hand over his in comfort then answered, "I'm up to the challenge with my information and technology network anything is possible. My current training was designed for a political career and your ideas match my own goals. I won't let you down."

"By the way, M.I. is really interested in that facial recognition software. Do you think your contact would be willing to share? Of course he would be compensated and receive full credit for his creations."

Kane tried to stifle a laugh and failed. Sam nudged him in the ribs and said, "I will have him contact M.I. in the next few days, Chancellor."

"We have arranged a private transport back to Pretoria that will be leaving in an hour. I'm sure you can't wait to get home to your family."

Sam couldn't hold back the tears and Robert answered. "Thank you, Chancellor." They rose to leave. "Will that be all?"

"Yes, but keep in mind we will be checking up on your progress.

"Understood, sir."

CHAPTER 24

THE TRIP home to Pretoria was uneventful. Sam had a lot of time to think about everything that happened. The implications were huge, a whole school dedicated to perfecting her gift and finding others with similar gifts. Nick was going to be excited that M.I. wanted his help not just his programs. *She could use Jamie right now. She needed some sleep these nightmares were driving her nuts*, she thought. Robert and Kane had been pouring over that file of operatives for hours, making all kinds of new list. They made plans to move quickly on the training center bombing first.

She was left alone with her thoughts and they strayed back to a conversation with C.J. He had stayed behind to pack up his house and would be arriving in a couple of days. He looked so happy when they left, like a kid given a special treat. He was telling Sam how he enjoyed coming to Pretoria on assignments, it gave him time to enjoy the fresh air and smell the flowers. He mentioned his headaches were less severe and he was interested in finding more about Jamie's herbal remedies. He would be staying at the Gabriels' home until suitable accommodations could be found.

Sam was given only enough time to call her parents before leaving Plutonus. Her mother sounded so relieved that she was okay and couldn't stop crying long enough to talk. Her father took the phone and sounded excited at the prospect of becoming a Chancellor. All his work for the alliance was finally paying off. He said she wouldn't believe the changes already on Pretoria. He told her of the e-mails pouring in from all over the planet. He had to start a new list of gifted citizens. He assured her that Jamie, Nick, and Niles knew she was okay and they would meet her when she landed.

Plans had been made to head directly home when she arrived. Everything would be handled from home until a security detail could be assigned to her. Her family would not be left unguarded while the rest of the cell members were apprehended.

She curled up in a chair, listened to her music, and tried to block events and get some sleep. She managed to sleep for a few hours, and then Robert brought over a plate of food. The aroma woke her from a deep sleep. Her stomach growled in response, and she sat up and took the plate from him. "Thanks. How much longer till we reach Pretoria?" She picked up her fork and started to eat.

"A few more hours and we'll be in the atmosphere. Before we reach there and we're engulfed with security, I want to talk to you." She put her fork down and pushed her plate away. She had a bad feeling about this conversation. "Finish eating first, please."

"I'm not hungry anymore. Just tell me what you have to say." She sniffed back the tears that were trying to escape and stiffened her spine for the inevitable blow. He took her hands in his and kissed each one. He looked into her eyes and smiled. She relaxed a little, but kept her defenses up.

"I want to see more of you when we reach Pretoria. We need to find out what is between us, when all this chaos isn't going on. Would you like that, Sam?"

She had been expecting him to tell her they couldn't continue what was going on, but this was unexpected. She wasn't sure what to say, all kinds of thoughts had been running through her mind.

If she didn't say something soon he might pour his heart out and he wasn't ready for that yet. She squeezed his hands tighter and finally put him out of his misery. "I want the same thing you do. No outside pressures just the two of us." He grabbed her and gave her a heart-stopping kiss that curled her toes.

"Break it up, you two." Kane stood behind them and laughed.

"Kane, if you don't go away I might have to kill you."

"Did you ever notice he's always right there to interrupt. It's like he has a sixth sense. Kane is there something you need to tell us?" Sam laughed.

"No, I just happen to be here at the right time."

"Don't you mean the wrong time?" Robert asked. They all laughed, and Sam thought it felt good to laugh again. After finishing her meal she curled up next to Robert and watched a movie. Things finally felt like they were getting back to normal.

"Colonel, we'll be arriving shortly, but there seems to be a problem."

Robert straightened in his seat "What kind of problem?"

"If you would look out the window you'll see what I mean." Sam couldn't believe the crowd that was gathered below. There had to be at least 1,000 citizens.

"What are they doing down there?"

"They're waiting for you, Miss Gabriels," Robert and Kane looked at each other and knew the answer.

"Sam, remember that e-mail virus Nick sent out? Your name was attached to it with the words 'Path to Freedom'. Nick wanted to make sure the right person got credit for the changes happening here on Pretoria. What do you want to do Sam?" Robert asked, taking her hand and linking his fingers with hers.

"Land here, please. I'll deal with Nick later. Two can play this game." As she spoke, her eyes turned emerald again.

"Officer, you heard the lady. Land here," Robert commanded.

"What about security?" He was looking nervously at the crowd gathered below.

"We're all the security she is going to need," Kane said with absolute authority.

They landed just outside the main terminal and the crowd gave out a loud cheer as the door opened and Sam appeared. Her family and friends rushed forward along with a number of security personnel. Niles stood to the side contemplating his grandpa's stories and shook his head in dismissal. *They couldn't be true*, he thought.

EPILOGUE

GRADUATION DAY

Chancellor Aron Gabriels was standing at the podium giving his speech. He emphasized the new direction for Pretoria's citizens better voting rights, new jobs, equal rights for all and recognition. He said action spoke louder than words and pointed out the newest facilities under construction. Sam, Jamie, Nick, and Niles sat at the head of the class. They were all graduating with honors. Sam barely listened to her father's speech. The following day she would begin her new job as head of Pretoria's School for the Gifted. There were many preparations to be finished before school started in the fall. Most of the incoming class would be from Luella and a few would be from Mantis. Future dorms would have to be built to accommodate the others traveling from a greater distance.

The teams of scientists were also anxious to get started; they had been hounding Jamie to join them. For her doctorate she had been working with Annie Gabriels hybridizing a new plant that could clean the air faster than trees could. Plutonus was monitoring their progress very closely in hope of a cure for their toxic air problem.

Military Intel had Nick very busy. They were not only using his facial recognition program but were paying him to create a new firewall program. They recently discovered he was not the only one able to get into their systems.

Niles has been assisting Robert and Kane, with his photographic memory. He has been able to uncover a whole network of hidden tunnels and passages throughout the planet. There was talk of Nick and Niles joining M.I. strictly on an as needed basis. They would both be given the rank of Lieutenant.

After Chancellor Lansing's e-mail, the remaining cell members scattered and the threat to the training center was aborted. Robert and Kane had been gathering a rather extensive number of cell operatives, but the last few were becoming difficult to find. Lynn Weston had wiped out a few too many memories, Kane and Robert found a number in the slums speaking gibberish.

C.J. was excited to begin his new life on Pretoria. He had agreed to be Aron's advisor and a teacher at the new school. His headaches were beginning to subside with help from Jamie's bag of tricks and the fresh air. Nick was able to track down C.J.'s parents. They would be arriving soon.

Barnabas Matthew and Frances Johnson had been handed over to CERT in hope of rehabilitation. It was last heard they were working in the mines, still arguing over who was at fault for the failure of the mission.

Sam was brought back from her thoughts as the applause began for her father. She was proud of his accomplishments. Over the previous couple of months he had spent traveling to Plutonus for meetings of the high council.

Kane and Robert were currently out on assignment and had missed graduation. Sam always worried he wouldn't return. She was sitting at a table in her parents' backyard with her friends when she felt his presence behind her. She jumped up into his waiting arms. "You're back!"

"We found the last cell member hiding in a farm house outside of town," He stepped back to admire her from head to toe not missing a thing. It was a good thing he stopped at home and changed before coming here. Kane nagged him on the way over about the way he dressed. He finally told Kane his mission. "You look beautiful. Come with me for a minute." He looked unsure until she nodded and he tugged her hand. Jamie was busy hugging Kane and missed the two walking away. Kane joined Nick and Niles at the table pulling Jamie down next to him and gave them all the details.

Robert pulled her along to her mother's flower garden where, in the middle surrounded by a hundred different scents, was an enormous fountain. He found the bench her father told him about and sat her down. He gathered her hands and looked into her emerald eyes. He took a deep breath and knelt on one knee like the knights of old, before her. "Sam we have been through a lot together. From the first day I saw you I knew there was something special between us. A day doesn't go by when you aren't in my thoughts. I was afraid to admit my feelings because I couldn't stand to have my heart broke. You see Sam, I love you," He pulled a black velvet box from his pocket and opened it to reveal an emerald and sapphire ring surrounded by five diamonds. "I had this ring made especially for you. The emerald and sapphire are interlaced and there is a diamond to represent each of our friends," Sam put a hand to her mouth as silent tears streamed down her face, she held out her left hand as he slipped on the ring. "Sam Gabriels, will you do me the honor of becoming my wife?"

She could only nod. "Yes! I love you too."

He gathered her into his arms, spun her around, and yelled, "She said yes!"

Loud cheers and whistles could be heard in the background. The soldier had found his enchantress.

LaVergne, TN USA
10 February 2010
172739LV00002B/1/P